NEW NOIR

NEW NOIR

JOHN SHIRLEY

First edition
First printing 1993

Published by Fiction Collective Two with support given by the English Department Publications Unit of Illinois State University, the English Department Publications Center of the University of Colorado at Boulder, and the Illinois Arts Council

Address all inquiries to: Fiction Collective Two, ℅ English Department, Publications Center, Campus Box 494, University of Colorado at Boulder, Boulder, CO 80309-0494

New Noir
John Shirley

ISBN: Paper, 0–932511–55–4

Produced and printed in the United States of America
Distributed by The Talman Company

Cover & text illustrations: Tim Ferret
Book design: Jean C. Lee

CONTENTS

Ferret © 1993

JODY AND ANNIE ON TV

First time he has the feeling, he's doing 75 on the 134. Sun glaring the color off the cars, smog filming the North Hollywood hills. Just past the place where the 134 snakes into the Ventura freeway, he's driving Annie's dad's fucked-up '78 Buick Skylark convertible, one hand on the wheel the other on the radio dial, trying to find a tune, and nothing sounds good. But *nothing*. Everything sounds stupid, even metal. You think it's the music but it's not, you know? It's you.

Usually, it's just a weird mood. But this time it shifts a gear. He looks up from the radio and realizes: You're not driving this car. It's automatic in traffic like this: only moderately heavy traffic, moving fluidly, sweeping around the curves like they're all part of one long thing. Most of your mind is thinking about what's on TV tonight and if you could stand working at that telephone sales place again...

It hits him that he is two people, the programmed-Jody who drives and fiddles with the radio and the real Jody who thinks about getting work...Makes him feel funny, detached.

The feeling closes in on him like a jar coming down over a wasp. Glassy like that. He's pressed between the back window and the windshield, the two sheets of glass coming together, compressing him like something under one of those biology-class microscope slides. Everything goes two-dimensional. The cars like the ones in that Roadmaster video game, animated cars made out of pixels.

A buzz of panic, a roaring, and then someone laughs as he jams the Buick's steering wheel over hard to the right, jumps into the VW Bug's lane, forcing it out; the Bug reacts, jerks away from him, sudden and scared, like it's going, "Shit!" Cutting off a Toyota four-by-four with tractor-sized tires, lot of good those big fucking tires do the Toyota, because it spins out and smacks sideways into the grill of a rusty old semitruck pulling an open trailer full of palm trees...

They get all tangled up back there. He glances back and thinks, *I did that.* He's grinning and shaking his head and laughing. He's not sorry and he likes the fact that he's not sorry. *I did that.* It's so amazing, so totally rad.

Jody has to pull off at the next exit. His heart is banging like a fire alarm as he pulls into a Texaco. Goes to get a Coke.

It comes to him on the way to the Coke machine that he's stoked. He feels connected and in control and pumped up. The gas fumes smell good; the asphalt under the thin rubber of his sneakers feels good. *Huh.* The Coke tastes good. He thinks he can taste the cola berries. He should call Annie. She should be in the car, next to him.

He goes back to the car, heads down the boulevard a mile past the accident, swings onto the freeway, gets up to speed—which is only about thirty miles an hour because the accident's crammed everyone into the left three lanes. Sipping Coca-Cola, he looks the accident over. Highway cops aren't there yet, just the Toyota four-by-four, the rusty semi with its hood wired down, and a Yugo. The VW got away, but the little caramel-colored Yugo is like an accordion against the back of the truck. The Toyota is bent into a short boomerang shape around the snout of the semi, which is jackknifed onto the road shoulder. The Mexican driver is nowhere around. Probably didn't have a green card, ducked out before the cops show up. The palm trees kinked up in the back of the semi are whole, grown-up palm trees, with the roots and some soil tied up in big plastic bags, going to some rebuilt place in Bel Air. One of the palm trees droops almost completely off the back of the trailer.

Jody checks out the dude sitting on the Toyota's hood. The guy's sitting there, rocking with pain, waiting. A kind of ski mask of blood on his face.

I did that, three of 'em, bingo, just like that. Maybe it'll get on TV news.

Jody cruised on by and went to find Annie.

It's on TV because of the palm trees. Jody and Annie, at home, drink Coronas, watch the crane lifting the palm trees off the freeway. The TV anchordude is saying someone is in stable condition, nobody killed; so that's why, Jody figures, it is, like, okay for the newsmen to joke about the palm trees on the freeway. Annie has the little Toshiba portable with the 12" screen, on three long extension cords, up in the kitchen window so they can see it on the back porch, because it is too hot to watch it in the living room. If Jody leans forward a little he can see the sun between the houses off to the west. In the smog the sun is a smooth red ball just easing to the horizon; you can look right at it.

Jody glances at Annie, wondering if he made a mistake,

telling her what he did.

He can feel her watching him as he opens the third Corona. Pretty soon she'll say, "You going to drink more than three you better pay for the next round." Something she'd never say if he had a job, even if she'd paid for it then too. It's a way to get at the job thing.

She's looking at him, but she doesn't say anything. Maybe it's the wreck on TV. "Guy's not dead," he says, "too fucking bad." Making a macho thing about it.

"You're an asshole." But the tone of her voice says something else. What, exactly? Not admiration. Enjoyment, maybe.

Annie has her hair teased out; the red parts of her hair look redder in this light; the blond parts look almost real. Her eyes are the glassy green-blue the waves get to be in the afternoon up at Point Mugu, with the light coming through the water. Deep tan, white lipstick. He'd never liked that white lipstick look, white eyeliner and the pale-pink fingernail polish that went with it, but he never told her. "Girls who wear that shit are usually airheads," he'd have to say. And she wouldn't believe him when he told her he didn't mean her. She's sitting on the edge of her rickety kitchen chair in that old white shirt of his she wears for a shorty dress, leaning forward so he can see her cleavage, the arcs of her tan lines, her small feet flat on the stucco backporch, her feet planted wide apart but with her knees together, like the feet are saying one thing and the knees another.

His segment is gone from TV but he gets that *right there* feeling again as he takes her by the wrist and she says, "*Guy*, Jody, what do you think I *am*?" But joking.

He leads her to the bedroom and, standing beside the bed, puts his hand between her legs and he can feel he doesn't have to get her readier, he can get right to the good part. Everything just sort of slips right into place. She locks her legs around his back and they're still standing up, but it's like she hardly weighs anything at all. She tilts her head back, opens her mouth; he can see her broken front tooth, a guillotine shape.

✣

They're doing 45 on the 101. It's a hot, windy night. They're listening to *Motley Crue* on the Sony ghetto blaster that stands on end between Annie's feet. The music makes him feel good but it hurts too because now he's thinking about *Iron Dream.* The band kicking him out because he couldn't get the solo parts to go fast enough. And because he missed some rehearsals. They should have let him play rhythm and sing backup, but the fuckers kicked him out. That's something he and Annie have. Both feeling like they were shoved out of line somewhere. Annie wants to be an actress, but she can't get a part, except once she was an extra for a TV show with a bogus rock club scene. Didn't even get her Guild card from that.

Annie is going on about something, always talking, it's like she can't stand the air to be empty. He doesn't really mind it. She's saying, "So I go, 'I'm *sure* I'm gonna fill in for that bitch when she accuses me of stealing her tips.' And he goes, 'Oh you know how Felicia is, she doesn't mean anything.' I mean—*guy*—he's always saying poor Felicia, you know how Felicia is, cutting her slack, but he, like, never cuts me any slack, and I've got two more tables to wait, so I'm all, 'Oh right poor Felicia—' and he goes—" Jody nods every so often, and even listens closely for a minute when she talks about the customers who treat her like a waitress. "I mean, what do they think, I'll always be a waitress? I'm *sure* I'm, like, totally a Felicia who's always, you know, going to be a *waitress*—" He knows what she means. You're pumping gas and people treat you like you're a born pump jockey and you'll never do anything else. He feels like he's really *with* her, then. It's things like that, and things they don't say; it's like they're looking out the same window together all the time. She sees things the way he does: how people don't understand. Maybe he'll write a song about it. Record it, hit big, *Iron Dream*'ll shit their pants. Wouldn't they, though?

"My Dad wants this car back, for his girlfriend," Annie says.

"Oh fuck her," Jody says. "She's too fucking drunk to drive, *any*time."

Almost eleven thirty but she isn't saying anything about having to work tomorrow, she's jacked up same as he is. They haven't taken anything, but they both feel like they have. Maybe it's the Santa Anas blowing weird shit into the valley.

"This car's a piece of junk anyway," Annie says. "It knocks, radiator boils over. Linkage is going out."

"It's better than no car."

"You had it together, you wouldn't have to settle for this car."

She means getting a job, but he still feels like she's saying, "If you were a better guitar player..." Someone's taking a turn on a big fucking screw that goes through his chest. That's the second time the feeling comes. Everything going all flat again, and he can't tell his hands from the steering wheel.

There is a rush of panic, almost like when Annie's dad took him up in the Piper to go skydiving; like the moment when he pulled the cord and nothing happened. He had to pull it twice. Before the parachute opened he was spinning around like a dust mote. What difference would it make if he *did* hit the ground?

It's like that now, he's just hurtling along, sitting back and watching himself, that weird detachment thing...Not sure he is in control of the car. What difference would it make if he *wasn't* in control?

And then he pulls off the freeway, and picks up a wrench from the backseat.

✣

"You're really good at getting it on TV," she says. "It's a talent, like being a director." They are indoors this time, sitting up in bed, watching it in the bedroom, with the fan on. It was too risky talking out on the back porch.

"Maybe I should be a director. Make *Nightmare On Elm Street* better than that last one. That last one sucked."

They are watching the news coverage for the third time on the VCR. You could get these hot VCRs for like sixty bucks from a guy on Hollywood Boulevard, if you saw him walking around at the right time. They'd gotten a couple of discount tapes at Federated and they'd recorded the newscast.

"...we're not sure it's a gang-related incident," the detective on TV was saying. "The use of a wrench—throwing a wrench from the car at someone—uh, that's not the usual gang methodology."

"Methodology," Jody says. "Christ."

There's a clumsy camera zoom on a puddle of blood on the ground. Not very good color on this TV, Jody thinks; the blood is more purple than red.

The camera lingers on the blood as the cop says, "They

usually use guns. Uzis, weapons along those lines. Of course, the victim was killed just the same. At those speeds a wrench thrown from a car is a deadly weapon. We have no definite leads..."

"'They usually use guns,'" Jody says. "I'll use a gun on your balls, shit-head."

Annie snorts happily, and playfully kicks him in the side with her bare foot. "You're such an asshole. You're gonna get in trouble. Shouldn't be using my dad's car, for one thing." But saying it teasingly, chewing her lip to keep from smiling too much.

"You fucking love it," he says, rolling onto her.

"Wait." She wriggles free, rewinds the tape, starts it over. It plays in the background. "Come here, asshole."

✣

Jody's brother Cal says, "What's going on with you, huh? How come everything I say pisses you off? It's like, *any*thing. I mean, you're only two years younger than me but you act like you're fourteen sometimes."

"Oh hey Cal," Jody says, snorting, "you're, like, Mr. Mature."

They're in the parking lot of the mall, way off in the corner. Cal in his Pasadena School of Art & Design T-shirt, his yuppie haircut, yellow-tinted John Lennon sunglasses. They're standing by Cal's '81 Subaru, that Mom bought him "because he went to school." They're blinking in the metallic sunlight, at the corner of the parking lot by the boulevard. The only place there's any parking. A couple of acres of cars between them and the main structure of the mall. They're supposed to have lunch with Mom, who keeps busy with her gift shop in the mall, with coffee grinders and dried eucalyptus and silk flowers. But Jody's decided he doesn't want to go.

"I just don't want you to say anymore of this shit to me, Cal," Jody says. "Telling me about *being* somebody." Jody's slouching against the car, his hands slashing the air like a karate move as he talks. He keeps his face down, half hidden by his long, purple streaked hair, because he's too mad at Cal to look right at him: Cal hassled and wheedled him into coming here. Jody is kicking Cal's tires with the back of a lizardskin boot and every so often he kicks the hubcap, trying to dent it. "I don't need the same from you I get from Mom."

"Just because she's a bitch doesn't mean she's wrong all the time," Cal says. "Anyway what's the big deal? You used to go along peacefully and listen to Mom's one-way heart-to-hearts and say what she expects and—" He shrugs.

Jody knows what he means: The forty bucks or so she'd hand him afterward "to get him started."

"It's not worth it anymore," Jody says.

"You don't have any other source of money but Annie and she won't put up with it much longer. It's time to get real, Jody, to get a job and—"

"Don't tell me I need a job to get real." Jody slashes the air with the edge of his hand. "Real is where your ass is when you shit," he adds savagely. "Now fucking shut up about it."

Jody looks at the mall, trying to picture meeting Mom in there. It makes him feel heavy and tired. Except for the fiberglass letters—*Northridge Galleria*—styled to imitate handwriting across its off-white, pebbly surface, the outside of the mall could be a military building, an enormous bunker. Just a great windowless...*block*. "I hate that place, Cal. That mall and that busywork shop. Dad gave her the shop to keep her off the valium. Fuck. Like fingerpainting for retards."

He stares at the mall, thinking: That cutesy sign, I hate that. Cutesy handwriting but the sign is big enough to crush you dead if it fell on you. *Northridge Galleria*. You could almost hear a radio ad voice saying it over and over again, "Northridge Galleria!...Northridge Galleria!... Northridge Galleria!..."

To their right is a Jack-in-the-Box order-taking intercom. Jody smells the hot plastic of the sun-baked clown-face and the dogfoody hamburger smell of the drive-through mixed in. To their left is a Pioneer Chicken with its cartoon covered-wagon sign.

Cal sees him looking at it. Maybe trying to pry Jody loose from obsessing about Mom, Cal says, "You know how many Pioneer Chicken places there are in L.A.? You think you're driving in circles because every few blocks one comes up...It's like the ugliest fucking wallpaper pattern in the world."

"Shut up about that shit too."

"What put you in this mood? You break up with Annie?"

"No. We're fine. I just don't want to have lunch with Mom."

"Well goddamn Jody, you shouldn't have said you would, then."

Jody shrugs. He's trapped in the reflective oven of the parking lot, sun blazing from countless windshields and shiny metalflake hoods and from the plastic clownface. Eyes burning from the lancing reflections. Never forget you sunglasses. But no way is he going in.

Cal says, "Look, Jody, I'm dehydrating out here. I mean, fuck this parking lot. There's a couple of palm trees around the edges but look at this place—it's the surface of the moon."

"Stop being so fucking arty," Jody says. "You're going to

art and design school, oh wow awesome I'm impressed."

"I'm just—" Cal shakes his head. "How come you're mad at Mom?"

"She wants me to come over, it's just so she can tell me her latest scam for getting me to do some shit, go to community college, study haircutting or something. Like she's really on top of my life. Fuck, I was a teenager I told her I was going to hitchhike to New York she didn't even look up from her card game."

"What'd you expect her to do?"

"I don't know."

"Hey that was when she was on her Self-Dependence kick. She was into Lifespring and Est and Amway and all that. They keep telling her she's not responsible for other people, not responsible, not responsible—"

"She went for it like a fucking fish to water, man." He gives Cal a look that means, *no bullshit*. "What is it she wants *now*?"

"Um—I think she wants you to go to some vocational school."

Jody makes a snorting sound up in his sinuses. "Fuck that. Open up your car, Cal, I ain't going."

"Look, she's just trying to help. What the hell's wrong with having a skill? It doesn't mean you can't do something else too—"

"Cal. She gave you the Subaru, it ain't mine. But you're gonna open the fucking thing up." He hopes Cal knows how serious he is. Because that two-dimensional feeling might come on him, if he doesn't get out of here. Words just spill out of him. "Cal, look at this fucking place. Look at this place and tell me about vocational skills. It's shit, Cal. There's two things in the world, dude. There's making it like *Bon Jovi*, like Eddie Murphy—that's one thing. You're on a screen, you're on videos and CDs. Or there's shit. That's the other thing. There's no *fucking thing in between*. There's being *Huge*—and there's being nothing." His voice breaking. "We're shit, Cal. Open up the fucking car or I'll kick your headlights in."

Cal stares at him. Then he unlocks the car, his movements short and angry. Jody gets in, looking at a sign on the other side of the parking lot, one of those electronic signs with the lights spelling things out with moving words. The sign says, *You want it, we got it...you want it, we got it...you want it, we got it...*

✣

He wanted a Luger. They look rad in war movies. Jody said it was James Coburn, Annie said it was Lee Marvin, but whoever it was, he was using a Luger in that Peckinpah movie *Iron Cross*.

But what Jody ends up with is a Smith-Wesson .32, the magazine carrying eight rounds. It's smaller than he'd thought it would be, a scratched grey-metal weight in his palm. They buy four boxes of bullets, drive out to the country, out past Topanga Canyon. They find a fire road of rutted salmon-colored dirt, lined with pine trees on one side; the other side has a margin of grass that looks like soggy Shredded Wheat, and a barbed wire fence edging an empty horse pasture.

They take turns with the gun, Annie and Jody, shooting Bud-Light bottles from a splintery gray fence post. A lot of the time they miss the bottles. Jody said, "This piece's pulling to the left." He isn't sure if it really is, but Annie seems to like when he talks as if he knows about it.

It's nice out there, he likes the scent of gunsmoke mixed with the pine tree smell. Birds were singing for awhile, too, but they stopped after the shooting, scared off. His hand hurts from the gun's recoil, but he doesn't say anything about that to Annie.

"What we got to do," she says, taking a pot-shot at a squirrel, "is try shooting from the car."

He shakes his head. "You think you'll aim better from in a car?"

"I mean from a moving car, stupid." She gives him a look of exasperation. "To get used to it."

"Hey yeah."

They get the old Buick bouncing down the rutted fire road, about thirty feet from the fence post when they pass it, and Annie fires twice, and misses. "The stupid car bounces too much on this road," she says.

"Let me try it."

"No wait—make it more like a city street, drive in the grass off the road. No ruts."

"Uh...Okay." So he backs up, they try it again from the grass verge. She misses again, but they keep on because she insists, and about the fourth time she starts hitting the post, and the sixth time she hits the bottle.

✣

"Well why *not?*" She asks again.

Jody doesn't like backing off from this in front of Annie, but it feels like it is too soon or something. "Because now we're just gone and nobody knows who it is. If we hold up a store it'll take time, they might have silent alarms, we might get caught." They are driving with the top up, to give them some cover in case they decide to try the gun here, but the windows are rolled down because the old Buick's air conditioning is busted.

"Oh right I'm sure some *7-11* store is going to have a silent alarm."

"Just wait, that's all. Let's do this first. We got to get more used to the gun."

"And get another one. So we can both have one."

For some reason that scares him. But he says: "Yeah. Okay."

It is late afternoon. They are doing 60 on the 405. Jody not wanting to get stopped by the CHP when he has a gun in his car. Besides, they are a little drunk because shooting out at Topanga Canyon in the sun made them thirsty, and this hippie on this gnarly old *tractor* had come along, some pot farmer maybe, telling them to get off his land, and that pissed them off. So they drank too much beer.

They get off the 405 at Burbank Boulevard, looking at the other cars, the people on the sidewalk, trying to pick some-one out. Some asshole.

But no one looks right. Or maybe it doesn't feel right. He doesn't have that feeling on him.

"Let's wait," he suggests.

"Why?"

"Because it just seems like we oughta, that's why."

She makes a clucking sound but doesn't say anything else for awhile. They drive past a patch of adult bookstores and a video arcade and a liquor store. They come to a park. The trash cans in the park have overflowed; wasps are haunting some melon rinds on the ground. In the basketball court four Chicanos are playing two-on-two, wearing those shiny, pointy black shoes they wear. "You ever notice how Mexican guys, they play basketball and football in dress shoes?" Jody asks. "It's like they never heard of sneakers—"

He hears a *crack* and a thudding echo and a greasy chill

goes through him as he realizes that she's fired the gun. He glimpses a Chicano falling, shouting in pain, the others flattening on the tennis court, looking around for the shooter as he stomps the accelerator, lays rubber, squealing through a red light, cars bitching their horns at him, his heart going in time with the pistons, fear vising his stomach. He's weaving through the cars, looking for the freeway entrance. Listening for sirens.

They are on the freeway, before he can talk. The rush hour traffic only doing about 45, but he feels better here. Hidden.

"What the *fuck* you doing?!" he yells at her.

She gives him a look accusing him of something. He isn't sure what. Betrayal maybe. Betraying the thing they had made between them.

"Look—" he says, softer, "it was a *red light*. People almost hit me coming down the cross street. You know? You got to think a little first. And don't do it when I don't *know*."

She looks at him like she is going to spit. Then she laughs, and he has to laugh too. She says, "Did you see those dweebs *dive*?"

✣

Mouths dry, palms damp, they watch the five o'clock news and the six o'clock news. Nothing. Not a word about it. They sit up in the bed, drinking Coronas. Not believing it. "I mean, what kind of fucking society *is* this?" Jody says. Like something Cal would say. "When you shoot somebody and they don't even say a damn word about it on TV?"

"It's sick," Annie says.

They try to make love but it just isn't there. It's like trying to start a gas stove when the pilot light is out.

So they watch *Hunter* on TV. Hunter is after a psychokiller. The psycho guy is a real creep. Set a house on fire with some kids in it, they almost got burnt up, except Hunter gets there in time. Finally Hunter corners the psycho-killer and shoots him. Annie says, "I like TV better than movies because you know how it's gonna turn out. But in movies it might have a happy ending or it might not."

"It usually does," Jody points out.

"Oh yeah? Did you see *Terms of Endearment*? And they got *Bambi* out again now. When I was a kid I cried for two days when his Mom got shot. They should always have happy endings in a little kid movie."

"That part, that wasn't the end of that movie. It was happy in the end."

"It was still a sad movie."

Finally at eleven o'clock they're on. About thirty seconds worth. A man "shot in the leg on Burbank Boulevard today in a drive-by shooting believed to be gang related." On to the next story. No pictures, nothing. That was it.

What a rip off. "It's racist, is what it is," he says. "Just because they were Mexicans no one gives a shit."

"You know what it is, it's because of all the gang stuff. Gang drive-bys happen every day, everybody's used to it."

He nods. She's right. She has a real feel for these things. He puts his arm around her; she nestles against him. "Okay. We're gonna do it right, so they really pay attention."

"What if we get caught?"

Something in him freezes when she says that. She isn't supposed to talk like that. Because of the *thing* they have together. It isn't something they ever talk about, but they know its rules.

When he withdraws a little, she says, "But we'll never get

caught because we just *do it* and cruise before anyone gets together."

He relaxes, and pulls her closer. It feels good just to lay there and hug her.

✣

The next day he's in line for his unemployment insurance check. They have stopped his checks, temporarily, and he'd had to hassle them. They said he could pick this one up. He had maybe two more coming.

Thinking about that, he feels a bad mood coming on him. There's no air conditioning in this place and the fat guy in front of him smells like he's fermenting and the room's so hot and close Jody can hardly breathe.

He looks around and can almost *see* the feeling—like an effect of a camera lens, a zoom or maybe a fish eye lens: Things going two dimensional, flattening out. Annie says something and he just shrugs. She doesn't say anything else till after he's got his check and he's practically running for the door.

"Where you going?"

He shakes his head, standing outside, looking around. It's not much better outside. It's overcast but still hot. "Sucks in there."

"Yeah," she says. "For sure. Oh shit."

"What?"

She points at the car. Someone has slashed the canvas top of the Buick. "My dad is going to kill us."

He looks at the canvas and can't believe it. "Mu-ther-*fuck!*-er!"

"Fucking assholes," she says, nodding gravely. "I mean,

you know how much that costs to fix? You wouldn't believe it."

"Maybe we can find him."

"How?"

"I don't know."

He still feels bad but there's a hum of anticipation too. They get in the car, he tears out of the parking lot, making gravel spray, whips onto the street.

They drive around the block, just checking people out, the feeling in him spiraling up and up. Then he sees a guy in front of a Carl's Jr., the guy grinning at him, nudging his friend. Couple of jock college students, looks like, in tank tops. Maybe the guy who did the roof of the car, maybe not.

They pull around the corner, coming back around for another look. Jody can feel the good part of the feeling coming on now but there's something bothering him too: the jocks in tank tops looked right at him.

"You see those two guys?" he hears himself ask, as he pulls around the corner, cruises up next to the Carl's Jr. "The ones—"

"Those jock guys, I know, I picked them out too."

He glances at her, feeling close to her then. They are one person in two parts. The right and the left hand. It feels like music.

He makes sure there's a green light ahead of him, then he says, "Get 'em both," he hears himself say. "Don't miss or—"

By then she's aiming the .32, both hands wrapped around it. The jock guys, one of them with a huge coke and the other with a milkshake, are standing by the driveway to the restaurant's parking lot, talking, one of them playing with his car keys. Laughing. The bigger one with the dark hair looks up and sees Annie and the laughing fades from his face. Seeing that, Jody feels better than he ever felt before. *Crack, crack.* She fires twice, the guys go down. *Crack, crack, crack.* Three times more, making sure it gets on the news: shooting into the windows of the Carl's Jr., webs instantly snapping into the window glass, some fat lady goes spinning, her tray of burgers tilting, flying. Jody's already laying rubber, fish-tailing around the corner, heading for the freeway.

✣

They don't make it home, they're so excited. She tells him to stop at a gas station on the other side of the hills, in Hollywood. The Men's is unlocked, he feels really right *there* as she looks around then leads him into the bathroom, locks the door from the inside. Bathroom's an almost clean one, he notices, as she hikes up her skirt and he undoes his pants, both of them with shaking fingers, in a real hurry, and she pulls him into her with no preliminaries, right there with her sitting on the edge of the sink. There's no mirror but he sees a cloudy reflection in the shiny chrome side of the towel dispenser; the two of them blurred into one thing sort of pulsing...

He looks straight at her, then; she's staring past him, not at anything in particular, just at the sensation, the good sensation they are grinding out between them, like it's something she can see on the dust-streaked wall. He can almost see it in her eyes. And in the way she traps the end of her tongue between her front teeth. Now he can see it himself, in his mind's eye, the sensation flashing like sun in a mirror; ringing like a power chord through a fuzz box...

When he comes he doesn't hold anything back, he can't,

and it escapes from him with a sob. She holds him tight and he says, "Wow you are just so awesome you make me feel so *good...*"

He's never said anything like that to her before, and they know they've arrived somewhere special. "I love you, Jody," she says.

"I love you."

"It's just us, Jody. Just us. Just us."

He knows what she means. And they feel like little kids cuddling together, even though they're fucking standing up in a *Union 76* Men's restroom, in the smell of pee and disinfectant.

✥

Afterwards they're really hungry so they go to a Jack-in-the-Box, get drive-through food, ordering a whole big shitload. They eat it on the way home, Jody trying not to speed, trying to be careful again about being stopped, but hurrying in case they have a special news flash on TV about the Carl's Jr. Not wanting to miss it.

The Fajita Pita from Jack-in-the-Box tastes really great.

✥

While he's eating, Jody scribbles some song lyrics into his song notebook with one hand. "The Ballad of Jody and Annie."

They came smokin' down the road
like a bat out of hell
they hardly even slowed
or they'd choke from the smell

Chorus:
Holdin' hands in the Valley of Death
(repeat 3X)

Jody and Annie bustin' out of bullshit
Bustin' onto TV
better hope you aren't the one hit
killed disonnerably

Nobody understands em
nobody ever will
but Jody knows she loves 'im
They never get their fill

They will love forever
in history
and they'll live together
in femmy

Holdin' hands in the Valley of Death

He runs out of inspiration there. He hints heavily to Annie about the lyrics and pretends he doesn't want her to read them, makes her ask three times. With tears in her eyes, she asks, as she reads the lyrics, "What's a femmy?"

"You know, like 'Living In femmy.' "

"Oh, infamy. It's so beautiful... You got guacamole on it,

you asshole." She's crying with happiness and using a napkin to reverently wipe the guacamole from the notebook paper.

✣

There's no special news flash but since three people died and two are in intensive care, they are the top story on the five o'clock news. And at seven o'clock they get mentioned on CNN, which is *national.* Another one, and they'll be on the *NBC Nightly News*, Jody says.

"I'd rather be on *World News Tonight*," Annie says. "I like that Peter Jennings dude. He's cute."

About ten, they watch the videotapes of the news stories again. Jody guesses he should be bothered that the cops have descriptions of them but somehow it just makes him feel more psyched, and he gets down with Annie again. They almost never do it twice in one day, but this makes three times. "I'm getting sore," she says, when he enters her. But she gets off.

They're just finishing, he's coming, vaguely aware he sees lights flashing at the windows, when he hears Cal's voice coming out of the walls. He thinks he's gone schizophrenic or something, he's hearing voices, booming like the voice of God. "*Jody, come on outside and talk to us. This is Cal, you guys. Come on out.*"

Then Jody understands, when Cal says, "*They want you to throw the gun out first.*"

Jody pulls out of her, puts his hand over her mouth, and shakes his head. He pulls his pants on, then goes into the front room, looks through a corner of the window. There's Cal, and a lot of cops.

Cal's standing behind the police barrier, the cruiser lights flashing around him; beside him is a heavyset Chicano cop who's watching the S.W.A.T. team gearing up behind the big gray van. They're scary-looking in all that armor and with those helmets and shotguns and sniper rifles.

Jody spots Annie's dad. He's tubby, with a droopy mustache, long hair going bald at the crown, some old hippie, sitting in the back of the cruiser. Jody figures someone got their license number, took them awhile to locate Annie's dad. He wasn't home at first. They waited till he came home, since he owns the car, and after they talked to him they decided it was his daughter and her boyfriend they were looking for. Got the address from him. Drag Cal over here to talk to Jody because Mom wouldn't come. Yeah.

Cal speaks into the bullhorn again, same crap, sounding like someone else echoing off the houses. Jody sees people looking out their windows. Some being evacuated from the nearest houses. Now an *Action News* truck pulls up, cameramen pile out, set up incredibly fast, get right to work with the newscaster. Lots of activity just for Jody and Annie. Jody has to grin, seeing the news cameras, the guy he recognizes from TV waiting for his cue. He feels high, looking at all this. Cal says something else, but Jody isn't listening. He goes to get the gun.

✣

"It's just us, Jody," Annie says, her face flushed, her eyes dilated as she helps him push the sofa in front of the door. "We can do anything together."

She is there, not scared at all, her voice all around him soft and warm. "It's just us," she says again, as he runs to get another piece of furniture.

He is running around like a speedfreak, pushing the desk, leaning bookshelves to block off the tear gas. Leaving enough room for him to shoot through. He sees the guys start to come up the walk with the tear gas and the shotguns. Guys in helmets and some kind of bulky bulletproof shit. But maybe he can hit their necks, or their knees. He aims carefully and fires again. Someone stumbles and the others carry the wounded dude back behind the cars.

Five minutes after Jody starts shooting, he notices that Annie isn't there. At almost the same moment a couple of rifle rounds knock the bookshelves down, and something smashes through a window. In the middle of the floor, white mist gushes out of a teargas shell.

Jody runs from the tear gas, into the kitchen, coughing. "Annie!" His voice sounding like a kid's.

He looks through the kitchen window. Has she gone outside, turned traitor?

But then she appears at his elbow, like somebody switched on a screen and Annie is what's on it.

"Hey," she says, her eyes really bright and beautiful. "Guess what." She has the little TV by the handle; it's plugged in on the extension cord. In the next room, someone is breaking through the front door.

"I give up," he says, eyes tearing. "What?"

She sits the TV on the counter for him to see. "We're on TV. Right now. We're on TV...".

Ferret • 1993

I WANT TO GET MARRIED, SAYS THE WORLD'S SMALLEST MAN!*

"You a fucking ho," Delbert said. "You don't come at me like that, not a fuckin ho."

"Fuck you, Delbert, who turned me out? You busted me out there on Capp Street when it was fucking 30 degrees—I ain' a motherfucking toss up like yo' nigger bitch cousins, I'm a white girl, motherfucker, I don't come out of that—"

"Don't be talkin that shit. You was already a fucking whore, you fucked that *ess ay* motherfucker CheeChee—"

"Sure so he didn't beat my fucking head in. Where were you? Where we you when he was slapping me and shit? Hittin' the fuckin' pipe, Delbert. Shit you knew what was going on—Where you going now goddamnit?"

Delbert was mumbling over the loose knob of the hotel room's door, trying to get out into the hall. The knob was about ready to come off. Brandy was glad Delbert was going

---

*The character herein referred to as "World's Smallest Man" is purely imaginary and is in no way related to anyone who may hold that title anywhere.

because that meant he wasn't going to work himself up to knocking her around, but at the same time she didn't want to be left alone, just her and the fucked-up TV that was more or less a radio now because the picture was so slanty you couldn't make it out, a two-weeks-old *Weekly World Inquirer*, and one can of Colt Malt stashed on the window ledge. And something else, he was going to get some money, maybe get an out-front from Terrence, and do some rock. She shouted after him, "You going to hit that pipe without me again? You suckin' it all up, microwavin that pipe, fuckin' it up the way you do it, and Terrence going to kick yo' ass if you smoke what he give you to sell—"

But he'd got the door open, yelling, "SHUT UP WOMAN I BITCH-SLAP YOU!" as he slammed it behind him with that soap-opera timing.

"*Fuck* you, you better bring me some fuckin..." She let her voice trail off as his steps receded down the hall. "...dope."

The fight had used her up. She felt that plunge feeling again, like nothing was any use so why try; and what she wanted was to go back to bed. She thought, maybe I get my baby out of Foster Care Hold, that place's just like prison. Shit Candy's not a baby anymore, she's ten, and she's half-white, looks more white than anything else, she'll be OK.

Brandy got up off the edge of the bed, walked across the chilly room, hugging herself, feeling her sharp hips under her fingers, as she went to the window. She looked out through the little cigarette-burn hole, just in time to see Delbert walk his skinny black ass out the front door, right up to Terrence. "The man's going to go off on you one of these days, Delbert, you be a dead nigger before you hit the emergency room, you fucking asshole," she said, aloud, taking satisfaction in it.

There was no reason, she thought, to be looking out the burn-hole instead of just lifting the shade; she didn't have anything to be paranoid about, there wasn't even any fucking crumbles of dope in the house, she hadn't had any hubba in two days, and now she was laying awake at night thinking about it, not wanting to go out and turn a trick for it because she had that really bad lady trouble, and the pain when they fucked her was like stabbing her pussy, the infection—

There it was, soon as she started thinking about it, the itching starts up bad again, itching and burning in her cunt. Ow Ow. Ow. Shit, go to the clinic, go to the clinic. She didn't have the energy. They made you wait so long. Treated you like a fucking whore.

She turned to the burn-hole again, saw Terrence walking along with Delbert, Terrence shaking his head. No more credit. Delbert'd be back up here, beat her till she'd hit the streets again. She turned away from the cigarette hole. Looking out through the tiny burn-hole was a tweakin' habit. Like picking holes in your skin trying to get coke bugs. Once she'd spent a whole day, eight hours straight staring out through that hole, picking her skin bloody, staring, turning away only to hit the pipe. That was when Delbert was dealing and they were flush with dope. Fucking cocaine made you tweaky, it was funny stuff. Maybe Delbert's cousin Darius would give her some. For some head. Her stomach lurched. She went back to the bed, looked again at the *Inquirer* article she'd been laboriously reading:

I WANT TO GET MARRIED,
SAYS WORLD'S SMALLEST MAN!

Ross Taraval, the world's smallest man, wants to get

married—and he's one eligible bachelor! He weighs only seventeen pounds and is only 28 inches high but he has a budding career as an entertainer and he's got plenty of love to give, he tells us. "I want a wife to share my success," said Ross, 24, who has starred in two films shot in Mexico, making him a star, or anyway a comet, in that enterprising land. Recently he was given a "small" role in a Hollywood film. "There's more to me than meets the eye," Ross said. "The doctors say I could have children—and I'd support my new wife in real style! And listen, I want a full-sized wife. That's what a real man wants—and I can handle her! Just let me climb aboard! I've got so much love to give and there's a real man inside this little body wanting to give it to the right woman!"

Ross, who was abandoned at three years old, was raised by Nuns in Miami. After attracting attention in the *Trafalgar Book of World Records,* Ross was contacted by his manager, six-foot-five-inch Benny Chafin, who could carry Ross in his overcoat pocket if he wanted to. Chafin trained Ross in singing and dancing and soon found him work in nightclubs and TV endorsements.

"I've got my eye on a beautiful house in the Hollywood hills for the right lady," Ross said.

There was a picture of the little guy standing next to his manager—not even coming up to the manager's crotch-height. The manager, now, was cute, he looked kind of like Geraldo Rivera, Brandy thought. There was a little box at the bottom of the article. It said,

If you think you'd be a likely life-mate for Ross and would like to get in touch with him, you may write him care

of the Weekly World Inquirer *and we'll forward your letter to him. Address your correspondence to...*

Huh. Stupid idea.

She heard Delbert's footsteps in the hall...

There was a stamp on the letter from her sister that hadn't been canceled. She could peel it off.

✣

"I think I got you a job at Universal Studios!" Benny said, striding breathlessly in.

"Really?" Ross's heart thumped. He climbed laboriously down off the chair he'd been squatting in to watch TV. The Sleepytime Inn had a Playboy Channel.

He hurried over to Benny, who was taking off his coat. It was May in Los Angeles, and sort of cold there. The cold made Ross's joints ache. Benny had said it was always warm in LA but it wasn't now. It was cloudy and windy.

It took Ross a long time to get across the floor to Benny, and Ross was impatient to know what was going on, so he started shouting questions through his wheezing before he got there.

"What movie am I in?" he asked. "Does it have Arnold Schwarzanegger?"

"Ross, slow down, you'll get your asthma started. No, it's not a movie. It's at their theme park. They want you to play King of the Wonksters for the tourists. It's a live show."

Ross stopped in the middle of the floor, panting, confused. "What're Wonksters?"

"They're...sort of like Eewoks. Little outer space guys. Universal's got a movie coming out about em at Christmas so this'd be next summer—if the movie hits—and—"

"Next summer! I need some work now! Those bastards! You said I could be in a buddy picture with Arnold Schwarzanegger!"

"I spoke to his agent. He already did a buddy picture with a little guy. He doesn't want to do that again."

"You said I could meet him!"

"You're going to be around Hollywood for a long time, you'll meet your hero, Ross, calm down, all right? You don't want to have an attack. Maybe we can get a photo op or something with him—"

Benny had turned away, was frowning over the papers in his briefcase.

"We're not even sleeping in Hollywood!" Ross burst out. He'd been saving this all morning, having heard it from the maid. "We're..."

"Hey, we're in LA OK? It doesn't matter where you live as long as you can drive to the studios. Most of em aren't actually in Hollywood anymore Ross, they're in Burbank or Culver City—"

"Mary, Mother of God! I want to go out in Hollywood! You're out getting wild with all the girls! No? You are! And leaving me here!"

Benny turned to him, his cheeks mottling. He cocked a hip, slightly, and Ross backed away. He knew, from when he was a boy the times he had run away from the Mission, how people stood when they were going to kick you.

He'd spent six weeks in the Mission hospital, after one kick stove in his ribs, and he wasn't quite right from it yet. He most definitely knew when they were going to kick you...

But Benny made that long exhalation through his nose that meant he was trying to keep his temper. He'd never kicked Ross, or hurt him at all, he probably never would. He'd done nothing but help him, after all.

"I'm sorry, Benny," Ross said. "Can we have a Big Mac and watch Playboy channel?"

"Sure. We deserve a break, right?" He'd turned back to his briefcase, sorting papers. "I had a letter here for you, from those people at the World Inquirer."

"I don't like those people."

"They're bloodsuckers. But the publicity is good, so whatever it is, we play along. We'll get a TV commercial or something out of it."

"I hope you are not mad at me, Benny..."

"I'm not mad at you. Hey, here it is. Your letter."

✣

There was something off about his face, Brandy thought. His nose seemed crooked or something. His features a little distorted. Must be from being a dwarf, or a midget, or whatever he was.

She tried to picture cuddling with him, think of him as cute, like a kid, but when she pictured him unzipping his pants, she got a skin-crawling feeling...

Hit the pipe a few times, anything's all right.

She pushed the pipe to the back of her mind. She had to play this carefully.

They were sitting in the corner booth of a Denny's restaurant. Ross, actually, was standing on the leatherette seat, leaning on the table like it was a bar, but the people who passed probably thought he was sitting. They also probably thought he was her kid. Shit, he was 28 inches high. His head, though, was almost normal sized. Too big for his body. He was wearing a stiffly pressed suit and tie, with a hanky tucked in the pocket; he looked like a little kid going to Sunday school. "Did a lot of women write to you?" she asked.

"Not too many. The ones that did are too big and fat or old, except you. Or they were black. I don't want a black wife. I liked you, because your hair is blond, and your letter was very nice, the handwriting was nice, the stationary was very nice. Smelled nice too."

But he was talking sort of distractedly. She could see he was staring at the scabs on her cheeks. There were only a few, really.

"I guess you're looking at my skin—" she began.

"No no no! It's fine. Fine." His voice sounded like it was coming through a little tube from the next room. He smiled at her. He had nice teeth.

"It's OK to notice it," Brandy said. "My...my sister has this crazy Siamese cat. You know how the little fuh—" Watch your language, she told herself. "You know how they are. I bent over to pet him and he jumped up and scratched me..."

Ross nodded. He seemed to buy it. Maybe where he was from they didn't have a lot of Hubba-heads picking at their skin all the time.

"There was a cat," he said absently, "who scared me, at the Mission. Big and fat and mean." He scowled and muttered something else in his munchkin voice she couldn't quite make out.

"It's nice of you to buy me dinner," Brandy said. A fucking Denny's, she thought. Well maybe it was like he said, it was just the nearest one and he was hungry. But she'd pictured some really fancy place...

The waitress brought their order, steak for Brandy—who knew if this was going to work out? Get what you can now—

and a milkshake and fries for the little guy, which was kind of a funny dinner, Brandy thought. The waitress had done a double take when she'd first come to take their order; now she didn't look at Ross directly. But she stared at Brandy when she thought Brandy wouldn't notice.

Fuck you, bitch, you think I'm sick for kickin' with the little dude.

"You really do look nice," Ross said, as the waitress walked away. Like he was trying to convince himself.

She'd done her best. Her hair was almost naturally blond, that was good, but it was a little thin and dry from all the hubba, and when she'd washed it, with that shitty hand-soap that was all Delbert had, it'd frizzed out, so she'd had to corn-row it. She'd handwashed her dress and borrowed Carmen's pumps and ripped off a pair of new pantyhose and some makeup from the Pavless drugstore. Getting the bus down here was harder, but she'd conned a guy at the San Francisco station into helping her out, and then she'd ditched him at the LA station when he'd gone to the men's room, and she'd got twelve dollars for the guy's luggage, so it was beginning to click.

Ross started to cough. "Are you choking on something?" she asked, dreading it, because she didn't want to attract even more attention.

"No—my asthma." He was fishing in his pocket with one of his little doll hands. He found an inhaler, and sucked at it.

"Just rest a bit, you don't have to talk or nothin," she said, smiling at him.

So his health was not that great. It wouldn't seem too weird or anything, then, if he died, or something.

✣

"You just swept me off my feet, I guess," Brandy said. "I thought you were hella cute at the wedding. I was surprised you didn't have your manager over to be, like, best man or something."

"We had to be married first, because I know what he would say, he doesn't want me to get married till he checks everyone out, you know. But *he* has lots of girls. Come on in, come on in, this is our room, our own room..."

"Wow, it even has a kitchen! Anyway, look, it's got a bar and a microwave and a little refrigerator..." She noticed that the microwave oven wasn't bolted to the wall. It was pretty old, though, she probably couldn't get shit for it.

"I do like this refrigerator, this little refrigerator by the floor. When we get a big house we'll have a real kitchen!"

"Yeah? Uhhh...When do you think—"

He interrupted her with a nervous dance of excitement, spreading his arms to gesture at the whole place. "You like this place? Las Vegas, it's so beautiful, everything's like a palace, all lit up, so much money, everything's like in a treasure chest."

"Uh huh." She started to sit on the edge of the bed, then noticed his eyes got all round and buggy when he saw her there. She moved over to the vinyl sofa, and sat down, kicked off her shoes. "It would've been nice if we coulda stayed in the Golden Nugget or one of them places—this Lucky Jack's is okay, but they don't got their own casino, they don't got room service..."

"Oh—we'll stay in the best, when Benny finds some work for me in Hollywood."

He toddled toward her, unbuttoning his coat. What did he think he was going to do?

She wondered where you got a rock in Vegas. She knew

there'd be a place. Crack cocaine is everywhere there's money. Maybe the edge of town out by the airport. She could find it. She needed the cash...

And then it hit her, and she stood up, sharply. He took several sudden steps back, almost stumbling. She looked down at him, feeling unreal. Had she been hustled by this little creature? "When Benny finds you some work? What do you mean?"

She felt the tightening in her gut, the tease of imagined taste in her mouth: the taste of vaporized cocaine and the other shit they put in it. She could almost feel the glass pipe in her hand; see the white smoke flowering in the glass tube, coming to her. Her heart started pounding, hands twitching, fuck, going on a tweak with no dope to hit, one hand picking at a scab on the back of her left forearm.

The little guy was chattering something. "Oh I'm working in Hollywood!" He actually puffed out his chest. "I'm going to star in an Arnold Schwarzanegger movie!"

"You mean you're going to co-star with him. OK. How much did you get paid?"

He fiddled with a lamp cord. "I don't have the check yet."

"Jesus fucking Christ."

He looked at her with his mouth open, so round and red and wet it looked like it had been punched in his head with a tool. "That is a blasphemy! That is the Lord's name! I can't have my wife talking like that!"

"Look—we're married now. We share everything right? *How* much we got to share? I need some cash, lover—for one thing, we didn't get a ring yet, you said we'd get a diamond ring—"

Ross was pacing back and forth, looking like a small child waiting for the men's room, trying not to wet his pants. "I don't have very much money now—thirty dollars—"

"Thirty dollars! Jesus fuh...that's a kick in the butt. What about credit cards?"

He wrung his little hands. Made her think of a squirrel messing with a peanut. "I'm paying with American Express for the airplane and hotel—Benny will stop the card!"

"American Express? Can you draw cash on the card?"

He stopped scuttling around and blinked up at her. "I don't know."

"Come on, we're gonna find out. We're going out."

"But we're Just Married!"

"It's not even dark out yet, Ross. Hold your horses, okay? First things first. We can't do anything without a ring, can we? We're gonna do something, don't worry. I'm hella horny. But we can't do it without a ring. That'd be weird don't you think?"

✣

When she came in, the little guy was sitting in the middle of the bed, with his legs crossed Indian style, in a pair of red silk pajamas. There was a Saint Christopher's medal around his neck. Probably couldn't get shit for that either.

It was after midnight, sometime. He had the overhead lights dialed down low, and the tall floorlamp in the corner was unplugged. In the dimness he looked like a doll somebody had left on the bed, some stuffed toy, till he leaned back on the pillow in a pose he'd maybe seen on the Playboy channel.

They'd got the limit for the account, three hundred cash on the American Express Card. They'd endured all the stares in the American Express office, and she'd kept her temper with the giggly fat guy who thought they were performing at Circus Circus, but the hard part had been making Ross swallow the *amazingly* bullshit story about how it was a tradition in California for the girl to go shopping for the ring alone...

She'd had to cuddle him and stroke his crotch a few times. His dick was a hard little thing like a pen-knife. Then she'd left him here with a bottle of pink Andre champagne, watching some shit about big-tit girls shooting each other with uzis. He'd made kissy faces at her as she left.

Right now, stoned, she thought maybe she could give him a blow job or something, if she closed her eyes. She had gone through two hundred fifty dollars in hubba, her mouth was dry as a baked potato skin from hitting the pipe.

"Let me see the beautiful ring on the beautiful girl," he said, his voice slurred. He said something else she couldn't make out as she crossed the room to him and sat on the bed, just out of reach.

"Hey, you know what?—Whoa, slow down, not so fast compadre," she said, fending his clammy little hands away.

She pointed at the girl on the wall-mounted TV screen; a girl in lavender lingerie. "How'd you like me to dress up like that, huh? I need something like that. I'd look hella good, just hella sexy in that. I know where I can get some, there's an adult bookstore that's got some lingerie, they're open all night, you can go in and look at movies and I'll—"

"No!" His voice was unexpectedly low. "I need you now!"

"Hey cool off—what I'm saying, you could call Benny and ask him to wire you some money. We need some things. He could send it to the all-night check-cashing place on Las Vegas Boulevard, they got Western Union—" She picked up her purse and went unsteadily toward the bathroom. The room was warped, because of the darkness and what the crack had done to her eyes. It always did weird shit to her eyes.

"Where you going?"

"Just to the bathroom, do some lady's business." I could tell him I'm in my period, Latin guys will steer clear from that, she thought. Maybe get another girl in here, give her a twenty to keep him occupied. "Why don't you call Benny while I'm in there, ask for some money, we need some stuff, hon!" She called, as she closed the bathroom door and fumbled through her purse with trembling fingers. Found the pipe, found the torn piece of copper scrubbing pad she was using for a pipe-screen, found the lighter. Her thumb was already blackened and calloused from flicking. Her heart was pounding in her ears as she took the yellowish white dove of crack from the inner pocket of the purse, broke it in half with a thumbnail, dropped it in the pipe bowl, melted it down with the lighter...

There was a pounding on the door, near her knee. She stared at the lower part of the door, holding the smoke in for a moment, then slowly exhaled. Her vision shrank and expanded, shrank and expanded, and then she heard, "You get out here and be with your husband!" Trying to make his voice all gravelly. She had to laugh. She took another hit. It wasn't getting her off much now. And she was feeling on the edge of that plunge into depression, that around the corner of the high; she felt the tweaky paranoia prod her with its hot icepick.

Someone was going to hear him yell; they were going to come in and see the pipe and she'd be busted in a Vegas jail. She'd heard about Vegas cops. Lot of times they raped the women they brought in. If they didn't like your looks, or you pissed them off more than once, they'd take you out to the desert and use you for target practice instead of highway signs or bottles, and just leave you out there...

"SHUT THE FUCK UP, ROSS!" she bellowed. Then thought: Oh great, that's even worse. She hissed: "Be quiet! I don't want anybody to come in here—"

"They were here, to bring towels, and they told me women don't go for the ring alone! That's not any kind of tradition! You come on out, no more little jokes!"

"*You're* a fucking little joke!" she yelled, as he started kicking the door. She turned the knob and slammed the door outward. Felt him bounce off it on the other side. Heard him slide across the rug, stop against the bedframe. A wail, then a shout of rage.

She thought again about a will. He might have more money stashed someplace, or some coming. But there was no way this thing was going to last out the night and she couldn't get him to a lawyer tonight and he was already suspicious. She'd have to just get his Rolex and his thirty bucks—twenty some now after the champagne—and maybe those little pajamas, sell that shit, no first get—

She paused to hit the pipe again. Part of her, tweakin', listened intensely for the hotel's manager or the cops.

—get that call through to his manager, make him give the manager dude some bullshit story, have him send the most cash possible. Maybe hustle a thousand bucks. Or maybe the little guy could be sold himself somewhere, Circus Circus or some place, or some kind of pervert. No, too hard to handle. Just make the call and then he should get a heart attack or something. He deserved it, he'd hustled *her*, telling her he had money, was a big star, but all the time he wasn't doing shit, getting her to marry him under false pretenses, fucking little parasite, kick his miniature ass...

A pounding low on the bathroom door again. Angrier now. The door was partly open. Little fucker was scared to put a limb through, but he stood to one side and peered in at her. "What is that? What is that in your hands? Drugs! Shit you're going to get us put in jail and you're going to ruin my career! It'll be a big scandal and Arnold won't want to be in a picture with me and—!" He had to break off for wheezing, and she heard him puff a couple of times on his inhaler, which was funny, how it was like her pipe.

She kicked the door open. He jumped back, narrowly avoiding its swishing arc. Fell on his little butt. For a moment she felt bad because he looked so much like one of her kids, then, like he was going to cry, and then for some reason that made her even madder, and she stepped out, pipe in one hand and lighter in the other, and kicked at him, clipping him on the side of the head with her heel. He spun, and blood spattered the yellow bedspread.

She paused to hit the pipe, melting another rock. Then she came slowly at him as she took a hit. Her mouth was starting to taste like the pipe filter more than coke, she wasn't getting good hits, she needed cash, get some cash and get a cab.

He was up on his feet, scuttling toward the door to the hall. He was just tall enough to operate the knob. There was no way she could let the little fucker go, and no way she was going to let the rollers get her in Vegas, fuck that. She crossed the room in three strides, exhaling as she went, trailing smoke like a locomotive, doing an end run around him, turning to block the door. He backed away, his face in darkness. He was making some kind of ugly hiccuping noise. He didn't look like a human being now, in the dimness and through the dope; he looked like some kind of little gnome, or like one of those little fuckers in that movie *Gremlins*, which was what he was like, some sneaky little thing going to run around in the dark spots and pull shit on you.

Maybe the microwave. If you didn't turn it up much it just sort of boiled things inside, it could look like he'd had a stroke. She had persuaded him to check in without her, they didn't know she was here. Unless he'd told the girl with the towels.

"You tell anybody I was here?"

He didn't answer. Probably, Brandy decided, he wouldn't have told much to some cheap hotel maid. So there was nothing stopping it.

He turned and scrambled under the bed. "That ain't gonna do you no good you little fucker," she whispered.

✣

Ross heard her moving around up there. He pictured her in a nun's habit. The nuns, when they were mad at him, would hunt him through the mission; he would hide like a rodent in some closet till they found him.

The dust under the bed was furring his throat, his lungs. He wheezed with asthma. She was going to get him into a corner, and kick him. She'd kick him and kick him with those hard, pointy shoes until his ribs stove in and he spit up blood. He tried to shout for help, but it came out a coarse whisper between wheezes. He sobbed and prayed to the Virgin and Saint Jude.

He heard her muttering to herself. He heard her move purposefully, now, to a corner of the room. He heard glass break. Surely someone would hear that and come?

What was she doing? What had she broken?

"Little hustlin' tight-ass motherfucker," she hissed, down on her knees now, somewhere behind him. Something scraped across the rug; he squirmed about to see. It was the tall floor lamp. She'd broken the top of it, broken the bulb, and now she was wielding it like an old widow with a broom handle trying to get at a rat, sliding it under the bed, shoving the long brass pole of it at him.

It was still plugged in. A cluster of blue sparks jumped from the bulb jags broken off in the socket as she shoved it at his face.

He tried to scream and rolled aside. The lopsided king's crown of glass swung to follow him, sparking. He could smell shreds of rug burning. He thought he could feel his heart bruising against his breastbone. She shoved the thing at him again, forcing him back farther...Then it stopped moving. She had moved away. Giggling.

Moving around the bed—

Ross felt her fingers close around his ankle. Felt himself dragged backwards, his face burning in the dusty rug; the back of his head smacking against the bed slats. He gave out a wail that tightened into a shriek of frustration, as she jerked him out from under the bed.

He clawed and kicked at her. She was just a great blur, a strange medicinal smell, big slapping hands. One of the hands connected hard and his head rang with it. He began to gag, and found himself unable to lift his arms. Like one of those dreams where you are trapped by a great beast, you want to run but your limbs won't work. She was carrying him somewhere, clasped against her, trapped in her arms like a dog to be washed.

He gagged again. Heard her say, from somewhere above, "Don't you fucking puke on me you little freak."

His eyes cleared. He saw she was carrying him toward a big box, open on this side. The place had an old, used, cheap microwave oven. The early ones had been rather big...

"Bennnnnyyyyyyyy!" But it never quite made it out of his throat.

In less than a second she had crammed him inside it He could feel his arms and legs again, feel the glass lining of the microwave oven against the skin of his hands and face; his head crammed into a corner, his cheek smashed up against the cold glass. He found some strength and kicked and she swore at him and grabbed his ankles in both her hands, stuffed his legs in far enough so she could press against his feet with the closing door. He could feel her whole weight against the door.

Crushed into a little box. A little box. Crushed into a little...

He pressed his palms flat against the glass, tucked his knees against his chest, deliberately pulling deeper into the oven. Felt her using the opportunity to close the door on him.

But now he had some leverage. He used all his strength and a lifetime of frustration and *kicked*.

The door smacked outward, banging against her chest. She lost her footing; he heard her fall backwards, even as he scrambled back and dropped out of the oven, fell to the floor himself, landing painfully on his small feet. She was confused, cursing incoherently, trying to get up. He laughed, feeling light-headed and happy.

He sprinted for the living room, jumping over her outstretched leg, and ran into the bedroom area. He could see the door, the way out, clearly ahead of him, unobstructed.

✣

Brandy got up. It was like she was climbing a mountain to do it. Something wet on the back of her head. The little fucker. The pipe. When had it got broken? It was broken, beside the sink. She grabbed the stem. It'd make a knife.

Shit—maybe the little fucker had already gotten out the door.

She felt her lip curl into a snarl, and ran toward the door—her ankle hooked on the wire stretched across the rug, about three inches over it, drawn from the bedframe to the dresser.

The lamp chord, she thought, as she pitched face first onto the rug. She hadn't left the cord that way...

The air knocked out of her, she turned onto her back choking, trying to orient herself.

The little fucker was standing over her, laughing, with the champagne bottle in his little hands; he clasped the bottle by the neck. A narrow bar of light came in between the curtains, spotlighting his round red mouth.

He was towering over her, from that angle, as he brought the champagne bottle down hard on her forehead.

✣

A BURGLAR KILLED MY NEW BRIDE!" SOBS WORLD'S SMALLEST MAN...The newlywed bride of Ross Taraval, the world's smallest man was murdered by an intruder on the first night of their Las Vegas honeymoon. Ross himself was battered senseless by the mystery man—and woke to find that his wife had been struck unconscious, raped, and murdered. Her throat had been cut by the broken glass of the drug-crazed killer's "crack" pipe. The burglar so far has not been located by police.

"It broke my heart," said the game little rooster of a man, "but I have learned that to survive in this world when you are my size, you must be stronger than other men! So I will go on...And I have not given up my search for the right woman, to share my fame and fortune..."

Ross hints that he's on the verge of signing a deal to do a buddy movie with his hero, Arnold Schwarzanegger. A big career looms up ahead for a small guy! "I'd like to share it with some deserving woman!" Ross says.

If you'd like to send a letter to Ross Taraval, the world's smallest man, you can write to him care of the Weekly World Inquirer, and we'll forward the letter on to him...

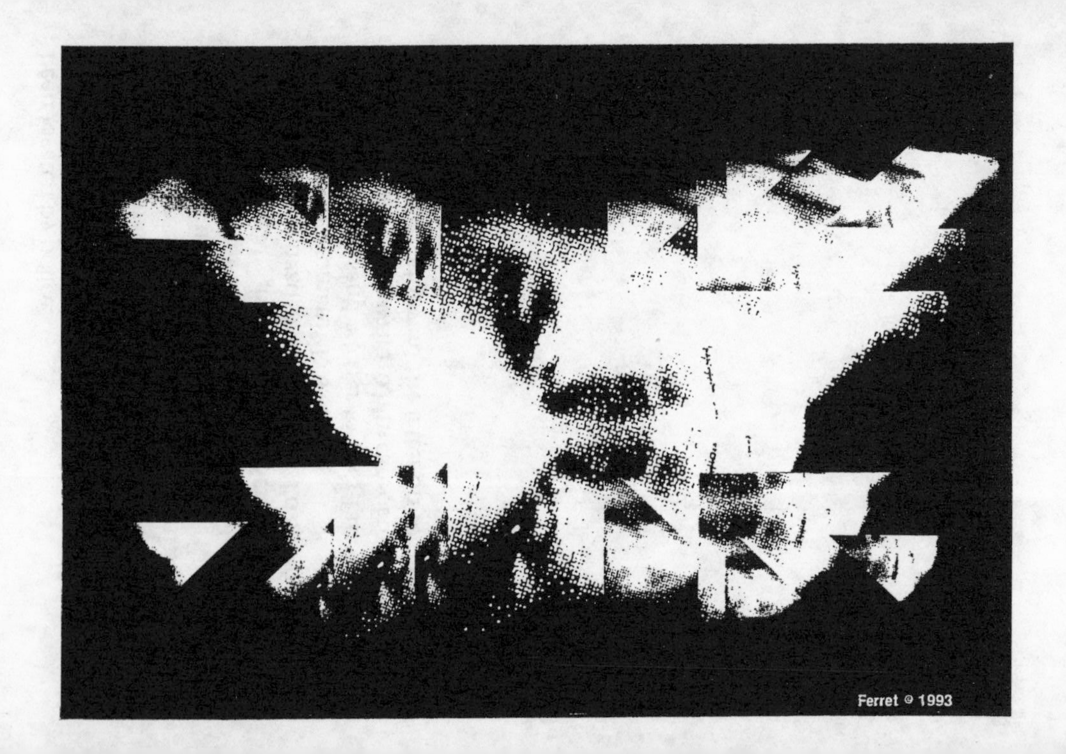
Ferret © 1993

EQUILIBRIUM

He doesn't know me, but I know him. He has never seen me, but I know that he has been impotent for six months, can't shave without listening to the news on TV at the same time, and mixes bourbon with his coffee during his afternoon coffee break and is proud of himself for holding off on the bourbon till the afternoon.

His wife doesn't know me, has never seen me, but I know that she regards her husband as "something to put up with, like having your period"; I know that she loves her children blindly, but just as blindly drags them through every wrong turn in their lives. I know the names and addresses of each one of her relatives, and whet she does with her brother Charlie's photograph when she locks herself in the bathroom. She knows nothing of my family (I'm not admitting that I have one) but I know the birthdays and hobbies and companions of her children. The family of Marvin Ezra Hobbes. Co-starring: Lana Louise Hobbes as his wife, and introducing Bobby Hobbes and Robin Hobbes as their two sons. Play the theme music.

I know Robin Hobbes and he knows me. Robin and I were stationed together in Guatemala. We were supposed to be there for "exercises" but we were there to help train the

Contras. It was a couple of years ago. The CIA wouldn't like it if I talk about the details, much.

I'm not the sort of person you'd write home about. But Robin told me a good many things, and even entrusted a letter to me. I was supposed to personally deliver it to his family (no, I never did have a family...really...I really didn't...) just in case anything "happened" to him. Robin always said that he wouldn't complain as long as "things turn out even." If a Sandinista shoots Robin's pecker away, Robin doesn't complain as long as a Sandinista gets *his* pecker blown away. Doesn't even have to be the same Sandinista. But the war wasn't egalitarian. It remained for me to establish equilibrium for Robin.

Robin didn't want to enlist. It was his parents' idea.

It had been raining for three days when he told me about it. The rain was like another place, a whole different part of the world, trying to assert itself over the one we were in. We had to make a third place inside the first one and the interfering one, had to get strips of tin and tire rubber and put them over our tent, because the tent fabric didn't keep out the rain after a couple of days. It steamed in there. My fingers were swollen from the humidity, and I had to take off the little platinum ring with the equal (=) sign on it. Robin hadn't said anything for a whole day, but then he just started talking, his voice coming out of the drone of the rain, almost the same tone, almost generated by it. "'They're gonna start up the draft for real and earnest,' my dad said. 'You're just the right age. They'll get you sure. Thing to do is, join now. Then you can write your own ticket. Make a deal with the recruiter.' My dad wanted me out of the house. He wanted to buy a new car, and he couldn't afford it because he was supporting us all, and I was just another expense. That was what renewed my dad, gave him a sense that life had a goal and was worth living: a new car, every few years. Trade in the old one. Get a whole new debt...My mom was afraid I'd be drafted too. I had an uncle was in the Marines, liked to act like he was a Big Man with the real in-the-know scuttlebutt; he wrote us and said the Defense Department was preparing for war, planning to invade Nicaragua, going to do some exercises down that way first...So we thought the war was coming for real. Thought we had inside information. My mom wanted me to join to save my life, she said. So I could choose to go to someplace harmless, like Europe. But the truth is she always was wet for soldiers. My uncle Charlie use to hang around in his dress uniform a lot. Looking like a stud. She was the only woman I ever knew who liked war movies. She didn't pay attention during the action parts; it wasn't that she was bloodthirsty. She liked to see them displaying their stripes and their braid and their spit and polish and marching in step, their guns sticking up...So she sort of went all glazed when Dad suggested I join the Army and she didn't defend me when he started putting the guilt pressure on me about not getting a job and two weeks later I was recruited and the bastards lied about my assignment and here I fucking am, right here. It's raining. It's raining, man."

"Yeah," I said. "It'd be nice if it wasn't raining. But then we'd get too much sun or something. Has to balance out."

"I'm sick of you talking about balancing stuff out. I want it to stop raining."

So it did. The next day. That's when the Sandinistas started shelling the camp. Like the shells had been waiting on top of the clouds and when they pulled the clouds away, the trap door opened, and the mortar rounds fell through...

✣

Immediately after something "happened" to Robin, I burned the letter he'd given me. Then I was transferred to the Fourth Army Clerical Unit. I know, deeply and intuitively, that the transfer was no accident. It placed me in an ideal position to initiate the balancing of Equilibrium and was therefore the work of the Composers. Because with the Fourth Clerical I was in charge of dispensing information to the families of the wounded or killed. I came across Robin Hobbes's report, and promptly destroyed it. His parents never knew, till I played out my little joke. I like jokes. Jokes are always true, even when they're dirty lies.

I juggled the papers so that Robin Hobbes, twenty years old, would be sent to a certain sanitarium, where a friend of mine was a Meditech who worked admissions two days a week. The rest of the time he's what they call a Handler. A Psych Tech. My friend at the sanitarium likes the truth. He likes to see it, to smell it, particularly when it makes him gag. He took the job at the sanitarium with the eighteen-year-old autistics who bang their heads bloody if you don't tie them down and with the older men who have to be diapered and changed and rocked like babies and with the children whose faces are strapped into fencing masks to prevent them from eating the wallpaper and to keep them from pulling off their lips and noses—he took the job because he *likes* it there. He took it because he likes jokes.

And he took good care of Robin Hobbes for me until it was time. I am compelled to record an aside here, a well-done and sincere thanks to my anonymous friend for his enormous patience in spoon-feeding Robin Hobbes twice daily, changing his bedpan every night, and bathing him once a week for the entire six months interment. He had to do it personally because Robin was there illegally, and had to be hidden in the old wing they don't use anymore.

Meanwhile, I observed the Hobbes family.

They have one of those new bodyform cars. It's a fad thing. Marvin Hobbes got his new car. The sleek, fleshtone fiberglass body of the car is cast so that its sides are imprinted with the shape of a nude woman lying prone, her arms flung out in front of her in the diving motion of the Cannon beachtowel girl. The doors are in her ribs, the trunk opens from her ass. She's ridiculously improportional, of course. The whole thing is wildly kitsch. It was an embarrassment to Mrs. Hobbes. And Hobbes is badly in debt behind it, because he totaled his first bodyform car. Rammed a Buick Sissy Spacek into a Joe Namath pickup. Joe and Sissy's arms, tangled when their front bumpers slammed, were lovingly intertwined.

Hobbes took the loss, and bought a Miss America. He is indifferent to Mrs. Hobbes's embarrassment. To the particularly judgmental way she uses the term *tacky*.

Mr. Hobbes plays little jokes of his own. Private jokes. But I knew. Mr. Hobbes had no idea I was watching when he concealed his wife's Lady Norelco. He knew that she'd want it that night because they were invited to a party and she always shaved her legs before a party. Mrs. Hobbes sang a little tuneless song as she quested systematically for the shaver, bending over to look in the house's drawers and cabinets, and *behind* the drawers and cabinets, peering into all the secret nooks and burrow-places we forget a house has; her search was so thorough I came to regard it as the product of mania. I felt a sort of warmth, then: I can appreciate...thoroughness.

Once a week, he did it to her. He'd temporarily pocket her magnifying mirror, her makeup case. Then he'd pretend to find it. "Where any idiot can see it."

Bobby Hobbes, Robin's younger brother, was unaware that his father knew about his hidden cache of Streamline racing-striped condoms. The elder Hobbes thought he was very clever, in knowing about them. But he didn't know about me.

Marvin Hobbes would pocket his son's rubbers and make *snuck-snuck* sounds of muffled laughter in his sinuses as the red-eared teenager feverishly searched and rechecked his closet and drawers.

Hobbes would innocently saunter in and ask, "Hey—you better get goin' if you're gonna make that date, right? Whatcha lookin' for anyway? Can I help?"

"Oh...Uh, no thanks, Dad. Just some...socks. Missing."

As the months passes, and Hobbes's depression over his impotence worsened, his fits of practical joking became more frequent, until he no longer took pleasure in them, but performed his practical jokes as he would some habitual household chore. Take out the trash, cut the lawn, hide Lana's razor, feed the dog.

I watched as Hobbes, driven by some undefined desperation, attempted to relate to his relatives. He'd sit them at points symmetrical (relative to him) around the posh living room; his wife thirty degrees to his left, his youngest son thirty degrees to his right. Then, he would relate a personal childhood experience as a sort of parable, describing his hopes and dreams for his little family.

"When I was a boy we would carve out tunnels in the briar bushes. The wild blackberry bushes were very dense, around our farm. It'd take hours to clip three feet into them with the gardener's shears. But after weeks of patient work, we snipped a network of crude tunnels through the half-acre filled with brambles. In this way, we learned how to cope with the world as a whole. We would crawl through the green tunnels in perfect comfort, but knowing that if we stood up, the thorns would cut us to ribbons."

He paused and sucked several times loudly on the pipe. It had gone out ten minutes before. He stared at the fireplace where there was no fire.

Finally he asked his wife, "Do you understand?" Almost whining it.

She shook her head ruefully. Annoyed, his jaws bruxating, Hobbes slipped on the floor, muttering he'd lost his tobacco pouch, searching for it under the coffee table, under the sofa. His son didn't smile, not once. His son had hidden the tobacco pouch. Hobbes went scurrying about on the rug looking for the tobacco pouch in a great dither of confusion, like a poodle searching for his rawhide bone. Growling low. Growling to himself.

Speculation as to how I came to know these intimate details of the Hobbes family life will prove as futile as Marvin's attempt to relate to his relatives.

I have my ways. I learned my techniques from other Composers.

Presumably, Composers belong to a tacit network of free agents the world over, whose sworn duty it is to establish states of interpersonal Equilibrium. No Composer has ever knowingly met another; it is impossible for them to meet, even by accident, since they carry the same charge and therefore repel from each other. I'm not sure just how the invisible Composers taught me their technique for the restoration of Equilibrium. To be precise, I *am* sure as to how it was done—I simply can't articulate it.

I have no concrete evidence that the Composers exist. Composers perform the same service for society that vacuum tubes used to perform for radios and amplifiers. And the fact of a vacuum tube's existence is proof that someone must have the knowledge, somewhere, needed to construct a vacuum tube. Necessity is its own evidence.

Now picture this: Picture me with a high forehead crowned by white hair and a square black graduation cap with its tassel dangling. Picture me with a drooping white mustache and wise blue eyes. In fact, I look a lot like Albert Einstein, in this picture. I am wearing a black graduation gown, and clutched in my right hand is a long wooden pointer.

I don't have a high forehead. I don't have any hair at all. No mustache. Not even eyebrows. I don't have blue eyes. (Probably, neither did Einstein.) I don't look like Einstein in the slightest. I don't own a graduation gown, and I never completed a college course.

But picture me that way. I am pointing at a home movie screen with my official pointer. On the screen is a projection of a young man who has shaved himself bald and who wears a tattered Army uniform with a Clerical Corps patch on the right shoulder, half peeled off. The young man has his back to the home movie camera. He is playing a TV-tennis game. This was one of the first video games. Each player is given a knob which controls a vertical white dash designating the 'tennis racket,' one to each half of the television screen. On a field of bland gray the two white dashes bandy between them a white blip, the 'tennis ball.' With a flick of the dial, snapping the dash/racket up or down, one knocks the blip past the other electronic paddle and scores a point. Jabbing here and there at the movie screen I indicate that the game is designed for two people. I nod my head sagely. But this mysterious young man manipulates left and right dials with both hands at once. (If you look closely at his hands, you'll note that the index finger of his left hand is missing. The index finger of his right hand is missing, too.) Being left-handed, when he first began to play himself, the left hand tended to win. But he establishes perfect equilibrium in the interactive poles of his parity. The game is designed to continue incessantly until fifteen points are scored by either side. He nurtured his skill until he could play against himself for long hours, beeping a white blip with euphoric monotony back and forty between wrist-flicks, never scoring a point for either hand.

He never wins, he never loses, he establishes perfect equilibrium.

The movie ends, the professor winks, the young man was at no time turned to face the camera.

My practical joke was programmed to compose an Equilibrium for Robin Hobbes and his family. Is it Karma? Are the Composers the agents of Karma? No. There is no such thing as Karma: that is why the Composers are necessary. To redress the negligence of God. We try. But in establishing the Equilibrium—something more refined than vengeance—we invariably create another imbalance, for justice cannot be precisely quantified. And the new imbalance gives rise to a contradictory inversity, and so the Perfect and Mindless Dance of equilibrium proceeds. For there to be a premise there must somewhere exist its contradiction.

Hence I present my clue to the Hobbes encrypted in a

reversal of the actual situation.

In the nomenclature of the composers, a snake symbolizes an octopus. The octopus has eight legs, the snake is legless. The octopus is the greeting the snake is the reply; the centipede is the greeting, the worm is the reply.

And so I selected the following document, an authentic missive illicitly obtained from a certain obsessive cult, and mailed it to the Hobbes, as my clue offered in all fairness; the inverted foreshadowing:

My dear, dear Tonto,

You recall, I assume, that Perfect and Holy Union I myself ordained, in my dominion as High Priest—the marriage of R. and D., Man and Wife in the unseeing eyes of the Order, they were obligated to seek a means of devotion and worship in accordance with their own specialties and proclivities. I advised them to jointly undertake the art of Sensual Communion with the Animus, and this they did, and still they were unsatisfied. Having excelled in the somatic explorations that are the foundation of the Order, they were granted leave to follow the lean of their own inclinations. Thus liberated, they settled on the fifth Degree in Jolting, the mastery of self-modification. They sought out a surgeon who, for an inestimable price, fused their bodies into one. They became Siamese twins; the woman joined to his right side. They were joined at the waist through an unbreakable bridge of flesh. This grafting made sexual coupling, outside of fondling, nearly impossible. The obstacle, as we say in the Order is the object. But R. was not content. Shorn of normal marital relations, R.'s latent homosexuality surfaced. He took male lovers and his wife was forced to lay beside the copulating men, forced to observe everything, and advised to keep her silence except in the matter of insisting on latex condoms. At first this stage left her brimming with revulsion; but she became aware that through the bridge of flesh which linked them she was receiving, faintly at first and then more strongly, her husband's impressions. In this way she was vicariously fulfilled and in the fullness of time no longer objected when he took to a homosexual bed. R.'s lovers accepted her presence, as if she were the incarnate spirit of the frustrated feminine persona which was the mainspring of their inner clockworks. But when their new complacency was established, the obstacle diminished. It became necessary to initiate new somatic obstacles. Inevitably, another woman was added to the Siamese coupling, to make it a tripling, a woman on R.'s left. Over a period of several months more were added, after the proper blood tests. Today, they are joined to six other people in a ring of exquisite Siamese multiplicity. The juncturing travels in a circle so the first is joined to the eighth, linked with someone else on both sides. All face inward. There are four men and four women, a literal wedding ring. (Is this a romantic story, Tonto?) Arrayed as they are in an unbreakable ring, they necessarily go to great lengths to overcome practical and psychological handicaps. For example, they had to practice for two days to learn how to collectively board D.'s Lear Jet. Four, usually the women, ride in the arms of the other four; they sidle into the plane, calling signals for the steps. This enforced teamwork lends a new perspective to the most mundane daily affairs. Going to the toilet becomes a yogic exercise requiring the utmost concentration. For but one man to pee, each of the joined must provide a precisely measured degree of pressure...They have been surgically arranged so that each man can copulate with the woman opposite him or, in turns, the man diagonal. Homosexual relations are limited to one coupling at a time since members of the same sex are diagonal to one another. Heterosexually, the cell has sex simultaneously. The surgeons have continuated the nerve ends through the links so that the erogenous sensations of one are shared by all. I was privileged to observe one of these highly practiced acrobatic orgies. I admit to a secret yen to participate, to stand nude in the center of the circle and experience flesh-tone piston-action from every point of the compass. But this is below my Degree; only the High Priest's divine mount, the Perfect and Unscrubbed *Silver*, may know him carnally...Copulating as an octuplet whole, they resemble a pink sea anemone capturing a wriggling minnow. Or perhaps interlocked fingers of arm wrestlers. Or a letter written all in one paragraph, a single unit...But suppose a fight breaks out between the grafted Worshippers? Suppose one of them should die or take sick? If one contracts an illness, all ultimately come down with it. And if one should die, they would have to carry the corpse wherever they went until it rotted away—the operation is irreversible. But that is all part of the Divine Process.

Yours very, very affectionately,
The Lone Ranger

✣

Mrs. Hobbes found the letter in the mailbox, and opened it. She read it with visible alarm, and brought it to her husband, who was in the backyard, preparing to barbecue the ribs of a pig. He was wearing an apron printed with the words, DON'T FORGET TO KISS THE CHEF. The word FORGET was almost obliterated by a rusty splash of sauce.

Hobbes read the letter, frowning. "I'll be goshdarned," he said. "They get crazier with this junk mail all the time. Goddamned pornographic." He lit the letter on fire and used it to start the charcoal.

Seeing this, I smiled with relief, and softly said: "Click!" A letter for a letter, equilibrium for the destruction of the letter Robin Hobbes had given me in Guatemala. If Mr. and Mrs. Hobbes had discerned the implication of the inverted clue I would have been forced to release Robin from the sanitarium to the custody of the Army.

When the day came for my joke, I had my friend bring Robin over to my hotel room which was conveniently two blocks from the Hobbes' residence.

It should be a harmless gesture to describe my friend, as long as I don't disclose his name. Not a Composer in face but one in spirit, my Meditech friend is pudgy and square shouldered. His legs look like they're too thin for his body. His hair is clipped close to his small skull and there is a large white scar dividing his scalp, running from the crown of his head to the bridge of his nose. The scar is a gift from one of his patients, given in an unguarded moment. My friend wears thick wire-rim glasses with an elastic band connecting them in the rear.

Over Robin's noisy protests I prepared him for the joke. To

shut him up I considered cutting out his tongue. But that would require compensating with some act restoring equilibrium which I had not time to properly devise. So I settled for adhesive tape, over his mouth. And of course the other thing, stuck through a hole in the tape.

Mr. Hobbes was at home, his Miss America bodyform car filled the driveway. The front of the car was crumpled from a minor accident of the night before, and her arms were corrugated, bent unnaturally inward, one argent hand shoved whole into her open and battered mouth.

Suppressing sniggers—I admit this freely, we were like two twelve-year-olds—my friend and I brought Robin to the porch and rang the doorbell. We dashed to the nearest concealment, a holly bush undulating in the faint summer breeze.

It was shortly after sunset, eight-thirty p.m. and Mr. Hobbes had just returned from a long Tuesday at the office. He was silent and grumpy, commiserating with his abused Miss America. Two minutes after our ring, Marvin Hobbes opened the front door, newspaper in hand. My friend had to bite his lip to keep from laughing out loud. But for me, the humor had quite gone out of the moment. It was a solemn moment, one with a dignified and profound resonance.

Mrs. Hobbes peered over Marvin's shoulder, electric shaver in her right hand; Bobby, behind her stared over the top of her wig, something hidden in his left hand. Simultaneously, the entire family screamed, their instantaneous timing perhaps confirming that they were true relatives after all.

They found Rob as we had left him on the doorstep, swaddled in baby blankets, diapered in a couple of Huggies disposable diapers, a pacifier stuck through the tape over his mouth, covered to the neck in gingham cloth (though one of his darling stumps peeked through). And equipped with a plastic baby bottle. The shreds of his arms and legs had been amputated shortly after the mortar attack on Puerto Barrios. Pinned to his chest was a note (I lettered it myself in the crude handwriting I thought would reflect the mood of a desperate mother.) The note said:

PLEASE TAKE CARE OF MY BABY

Ferret © 1993

SKEETER JUNKIE

It struck him, then, and powerfully. How consummate, how exquisite: A mosquito.

Look at the thing. No fraction of it wasted or distracted; more streamlined than any fighter jet, more elegant, for Hector Ansia's taste, than any sports car; in that moment, sexier—and skinnier—than any fashion model. A mosquito.

Hector was happily watching the mosquito penetrate the skin of his right arm.

He was in his El Paso studio apartment, wearing only his threadbare Fruit of the Loom briefs because the autumn night was hot and sticky. The place was empty except for a few books and busted coffee table and sofa, the only things he hadn't been able to sell. But as soon as he'd slammed the heroin, the rat-hole apartment had transformed into a palace bedroom, his dirty sofa into new silk cushions, the heavy, polluted air became the zephyrs of Eden, laced with incense. It wasn't that he hallucinated things that weren't there; but what was there had recast into a heroin-polished dimension of excellence. As he'd taken his shot, he'd looked out the windows at the refineries that studded the periphery of El Paso, through the lens of heroin transformed into Disney castles, their burn-off flames the torches of some charming medieval festival.

He'd just risen out of his nod, like a balloon released under heavy water, ascending from a zone of sweet weight to a place of sweet buoyancy, and he'd only now opened his eyes, and the first thing he saw was the length of his arm over the side of the old velvet sofa. The veins were distended because of the pressure on the underside of his arm, and halfway between his elbow and his hand was the mosquito, pushing its organic needle through the greasy raiment of his epidermis...

It was so fine.

He hoped the mosquito could feel the sun of benevolence that pulsed in him. The china white was good, especially because he'd had a long and cruel sickness before finding it, and he'd been maybe halfway to clean again, so his tolerance was down, and that made it so much better to hit the smack in, to fold it into himself.

Stoned, he could feel his Mama's hands on him. He was three years old, and she was washing his back as he sat in a warm bath, and sometimes she would kiss the top of his head. He could feel it now. That's what heroin gave him back.

She hadn't touched him after his fourth birthday, when her new boyfriend had come in fucked up on reds and wine, and the boyfriend had kicked Mama in the head and called her a whore, and the kick broke something in her brain, and after that she just looked at him blank when he cried...Just looked at him...

Heroin took him back, before his fourth birthday. Sometimes all the way back.

Look at that skeeter, now. Made Hector want to fuck, looking at it.

The mosquito was fucking his arm, wasn't it? Sure it was. Working that thing in. A proboscis, what it was called.

He could feel a thudding from somewhere. After a long moment he was sure the thudding wasn't his pulse; it was the radio downstairs. Lulu, listening to the radio.

Lulu had red-blond hair, cut like in the style of English girls from the old *Beatles* movies, its points near her cheeks curled to aim at her full lips. She had wide hips and round arms and hazel eyes. He'd talked to her in the hall and she'd been kind of pityingly friendly, enough to pass the time for maybe a minute, but she wouldn't go out with him, or even come in for coffee. Because she knew he was a junkie. Everyone on Selby Avenue knew a junkie when they saw them. He could tell her about his Liberal Arts B.A., but it wouldn't matter: he'd still be just a junkie to her. No use trying to explain, a degree didn't get you a life anymore, there wasn't any work anyway, you might as well draw your SSI and sell your food stamps; you might as well be a junkie.

Lulu probably figured if she got involved with Hector, he'd steal her money, and maybe give her AIDS. She was wrong about the AIDS—he never ever shared needles—but she was right he'd steal her money, of course. The only reason he hadn't broken into her place was because he knew she'd never leave any cash there, or anything valuable, not living downstairs from a junkie. He'd never get even a ten dollar bag out of that crappy little radio he'd seen through the open door. Nothing much in there. Posters of Chagall, a framed photo of Sting, succulents overflowing clay pots shaped like burros and turtles.

She was succulent; he wanted her almost as much as her paycheck.

He watched the mosquito.

If he lifted his arm up, would the mosquito stop drinking? He hoped not. He could feel a faint ghost of a pinch, a sensation he saw in his mind's eye as a rose bud opening, and opening, and opening, more than any rose ever had petals.

Careful. He swung his feet on the floor, without moving his arm. The mosquito didn't stir. Then he lifted the arm up, very, very slowly, inch by inch, so as not to disturb the mosquito. It kept right on drinking.

With excruciating languor, Hector stood up straight, keeping the arm motionless except for the slow, slow act of standing. Then—walking *very* carefully, because the dope made the floor feel like a trampoline—he went to the bookshelf. Easing his right hand onto the edge of a shelf to keep the arm steady, he ran his left over the dusty tops of the old encyclopedia set. He was glad no one had bought it, now.

The lettering on the book-backs oozed one word onto the next. He was pretty loaded. It was good stuff. He forced his eyes to focus, and then pulled the *M* book out.

Moving just as slowly, his right arm ramrod stiff, so as not to disturb his beloved—the communion pinch, his precious guest—he returned to the sofa. He sat down, his right arm propped on the arm of the sofa, his left hand riffling pages.

Mosquito...

(There was another shot ready on the coffee table. Not yet, pendajo. Make it last).

...the female mosquito punctures the skin with equipment contained in a proboscis, comprised of six elongated stylets. One stylet is an inverted trough; the rest are slender mandibles, maxillae, and a stylet for the injection of mosquito saliva. These latter close the trough to make a rough tube. After insertion, the tube arches so that the tip can probe for blood about half a millimeter beneath the epidermal surface...Two of the stylets are

serrated and saw through the tissue for the others. If a pool of blood forms in a pocket of laceration the mosquito ceases movement and sucks the blood with two pumps located in her head...

Mosquito saliva injected while probing prevents blood clotting and creates the itching and swelling accompanying a bite...

Hector soaked up a pool of words here, a puddle there, and the color pictures—how wonderfully they put together encyclopedias!—and then he let the volume slide off his lap onto the floor, and found the other syringe with his left hand, and, hardly having to look, with the ambidexterity of a needle freak, shot himself up in a vein he was saving, in his right thigh. All the time not disturbing the mosquito.

He knew it was too big a load. But he'd had that long, long jones, like mirrors reflecting into one another. It should be all right. He stretched out on the sofa again as the hit melted through him, and focused on the mosquito.

Hector's eyelids slid almost shut. But that worked like adjusting binoculars. Making the mosquito come in closer, sharper. It was like he was seeing it under a microscope now. Like he was standing—no, floating—floating in front of the mosquito and he was smaller than it was, like a man standing by an oil derrick, watching it pump oil up from the deep places, the zone of sweet weight...thirty-weight, ha...An *Anopheles gambiae* this variety. From this magnified perspective the mosquito's parts were rougher than they appeared from the human level—there were bristles on her head, slicked back like stubby oiled hair, and he could see that the sheath-like covering of the proboscis had fallen in a loop away from the stylets...her tapered golden body, resting on the long, translucent, frail-looking legs, cantilevered forward to drink, as if in obeisance...her rear lifted, a forty degree angle from the skin, its see-through abdomen glowing red with blood like a little Christmas light...

...it is the female which bites, her abdomen distends enormously, allowing her to take in as much as four times her weight in blood...

He had an intimate relationship with this mosquito. It was *entering* him. He could feel her tiny, honed mind, like one of those minute paintings obsessed hobbyists put on the head of a pin. He sensed her regard. The mosquito was dimly aware of his own mind hovering over her. He could close in on the tiny gleam of her insect mind—less than the "mind" of an electric watch—and replace it with his own. What a rare and elegant nod that would be: getting into her head so he could feel what it was like to drink his own blood through the slender proboscis...

He could do it. He could superimpose himself and fold his own consciousness up into the micro-cellular spaces. Any mind, large or small, could be concentrated in microscopic space; microspace was as infinite, downwardly, as interstellar space, wasn't it? God experienced every being's consciousness. God's mind could fit into a mosquito. Like all that music on a symphony going through the needle of a record player, or through the tiny laser of a CD. The stylet in the mosquito's proboscis was like the record player's stylus...

He could circle, and close in, and participate, and become. He could...

...see the rising fleshtone of his own arm stretching out in front of him, a soft ridge of topography. He could see the glazing eyes of the man he was drinking from. Himself; perhaps formerly. It was a wonderfully malevolent miracle: he was inside the mosquito. He was the mosquito. Its senses altered and enhanced by his own more-evolved prescience.

His blood was a syrup. The mosquito didn't taste it, as such; but Hector could taste it—through his psychic extension of the mosquito's senses, he supposed—and there were many confluent tastes in it, mineral and meat and electrically charged waters and honeyed glucose and acids and hemoglobin. And very faintly, heroin. His eggs would be well sustained—

Her eggs. Keep your identity sorted out. Better yet, set your own firmly atop hers. Take control.

Stop drinking.

More.

No. Insist, Hector. Who's in charge, here? Stop drinking and fly. Just imagine! To take flight—

Almost before the retraction of her proboscis was completed, he was in the air, making the wings work without having to think about it. When he tried too hard to control the flight, he foundered; so he simply flew.

His flight path was a herky-jerky spiral, each geometric section of it a portion of an equation.

His senses expanded to adjust to the scope of his new possibilities of movement: the great cavern, the massive organism at the bottom of it: himself, Hector's human body, left behind.

Hector sensed a temperature change, a nudge of air: a current from the crack in the window. He pushed himself up the stream, increasing his wing energy, and thought: *I'll crash on the edges of the glass, it's a small crack...*

But he let the insect's navigational instincts hold sway, and he was through, and out into the night.

He could go anywhere, anywhere at all...

He went downstairs.

Her window was open.

✣

From a distance, the landscape of Lulu was glorious, lying there on the couch in her bikini underpants, and nothing else. Her exposed breasts were great slack mounds of cream and cherry. She'd fallen asleep with the radio on; there were three empty cans of beer on the little end table by her head. One of her legs was drawn up, tilted to lean its knee against the wall, the other out straight, the limbs apart enough to trace her open labia against the blue silk panties.

Hector circled near the ceiling. The radio was a distorted boom of taffied words and industrial-sized beat, far off to port. He thought that, just faintly, he could actually feel radio and TV waves washing over him, passing through the air.

He wanted Lulu. She *looked* asleep. But suppose she felt him, suppose she heard the whine of his coming, and slapped, perhaps just in reflex, and crushed him—

Would he die when the mosquito died?

Maybe that would be all right.

Hector descended to her, following the broken geometries of insect flight-path down, an aerialist's unseen staircase, asymmetrical and yet perfect.

Closer—he could feel her heat. God, she was like a lake of fire! How could the skeeters bear it?

He entered her atmosphere. That's how it seemed: she was almost planetary in her glowing vastness, hot-house and fulsome. He descended through hormone-rich layers of her atmosphere, to deeper and more personal heats, until he'd settled on the skin of her left leg, near the knee.

Jesus! It was revolting. It was ordinary human skin.

But up this close; hugely magnified by his mosquito's

perspective...

It was a cratered landscape, orange and gold and in places leprous-white; here and there flakes of blue, where dead skin cells were shedding away. In the wens of pores and around the bases of the occasional stiff stalks of hair were puddly masses of pasty stuff he guessed were colonies of bacteria. The skin itself was textured like pillows of meat all sewn together. The smells off it were overwhelming: rot and uric acid and the various compounds in sweat and a chemical smell of something she'd bathed with—and an exudation of something she'd been eating...

Hector was an experienced hand with drugs; he shifted his viewpoint from revulsion to obsession, to delight in the yeasty completeness of this immersion in the biological essence of her. And there was another smell that came to him then, affecting him the way the sight of a woman's cleavage had, in his boyhood. Blood.

Unthinking, he had already allowed the mosquito to unsheath their stylets and drive them into a damp pillow of skin cells. He pushed, rooted, moving the slightly arched piercer in a motion that outlined a cone, breaking tiny capillaries just inside the epidermis, making a pocket for the blood to pool in. And injecting the anti-coagulant saliva.

Her blood was much like his, but he could taste the femaleness of it, the hormonal signature and...alcohol.

She swatted him.

He felt the wind of the giant hand, before it struck. She struck at him in her sleep, and the hand wasn't rigid enough to hit him; the palm was slightly cupped. But the hand covered Hector like a lid, for a moment.

The air pressure flattened the mosquito, and Hector feared for his spindly legs, but then light flashed over him again and the lid lifted, and he withdrew and flew, wings whining, up a short distance into the air...

She was mostly quiescent now. Looking from here like the rolling, shrub-furred hills you saw in parts of California: one hill blending smoothly into the next, until you got close and saw ant colonies and rattlers and tarantulas between the clumps.

She hadn't awakened. And from up here her thighs looked so sweet and tender...

He dipped down, and alighted on Lulu's left inside thigh, not far from the pale blue circus tent billow of her panties. The material was only a little stained; he could see the tracery of' her labia like the shadows of sleeping dragons under a silk canopy. The thigh skin was a little smoother, paler. He could see the woods of pubic hair down the slope a little.

Enough. Eggs, outside.

No. He was in control. He was going to get closer...

When at last he reached the frontier of Lulu's panties, and stood between two outlying spring-shaped stalks of red-brown pubic hair, gazing under a wrinkle in the elastic at the monumental vertical furrow of her vaginal lips, he was paralyzed by fear. This was a great temple to some sub-aquatic monster, and would surely punish any intrusion.

With the fear came a sudden perception of his own relative tininess, now, and an unbottling of his resentments. She was forbidden; she was gargantuan in both size and arrogance.

But he had learned that he was the master of his reality: he had found a hatch in his brain, and a set of new controls that fit naturally to his grip, and he could remake his being as he chose.

A sudden darkness, then; a wind—

He sprang up, narrowly escaping the swat. Hearing a sound like a jet breaking the sound barrier—the wind of her hand and the slap on her thigh. Then a murky roaring, a boulder-fall of misshapen words. The goddess coming awake; the goddess speaking.

Something like, *"Fucking skeeter...little shit...get the fuck out..."*

Oh, yes?

The fury swelled in him, and as it grew—Lulu shrank. Or seemed to, as rage pushed his boundaries outward like hot air in a parade balloon, but unthinkably fast. She shrank to woman size, once more in perspective and once more desirable.

She screamed, of course.

He glimpsed them both in her vanity mirror...

A man-sized mosquito, poised over her, holding her down with slender but strong front legs; Lulu screaming, thrashing, as he leaned back onto his hind legs and spread her legs with the middle limbs and drove his piercer through the fabric of her panties and into the forbidden temple of the goddess, into the tube of what was now only the tender little outer membrane of her reproductive organs. He thrust the thirty-inch proboscal stylets deep into the vagina. He pulled out a little; he thrust in...feeling her writhe in a disgusted ecstasy...

He might go the next step. Thrust through her cervix, into the womb, and beyond to an artery; suck her so hard she turned inside out and atomized and sucked whole into him, making him three times bigger.

But he held off. He pumped his proboscis like a dick and—

In her delighted revulsion, she struck at the mosquito's compound eyes.

The pain was realer and more personal than he'd expected. He jerked back, withdrawing, floundering off the edge of the bed, feeling a leg shatter against the floor and a wing crack, one of his eyes half blind...

The pain and the disorientation unmanned him. Emasculated him, intimidated him. As always when that happened, he shrank.

The boundaries of the room expanded and the bed grew, around him, into a dirty white plain; Lulu grew, again becoming a small world to herself...Her hand sliced down at him—

He threw himself frantically into the air, his damaged wings ascending stochastically; the wings' keening sound not quite right now, his trajectory uncertain.

The ceiling loomed; the window crack beckoned.

In seconds he had swum upstream against the night air, and managed to aim himself between the edges of the crack in the glass; the lips of the break like a crystalline take on her vagina. Then he was out into the night, and regaining some greater control over his wings...

That's not how it was, he realized: *she,* the mosquito had control. That's how they'd gotten through the crack and out into the night.

Let the mosquito mind take the head, then, for now, while he rested his psyche and pondered. That great yellow egg, green around the edges with refinery toxins, must be the moon; this jumble of what seemed skyscraper-sized structures must be the pipes and chimneys and discarded tar buckets of the apartment building's roof.

Something washed over him, rebounding, making him shudder in the air. Only after it departed did it register in his hearing: a single high note, from somewhere above.

There, it came again, more defined and pulsingly closer, as if growing in an alien certainty about its purpose.

The mosquito redoubled its wing beats in reaction, and there was an urgency that was too neurologically primitive to be actual fear. *Enemy. Go.*

Hector circled down between the old brick apartment buildings, toward the streetlight...

Another, slightly higher, even more purposeful note hit Hector, resonating him, and then a shadow draped him, and wing beats thudded tympanically on the air. He saw the bat for one snapshot-clear moment, superimposed against the dirty indigo sky. Hector knew he should detach from the mosquito, but the outspread wings of the bat, its pointed ears and wet snout, caught him with its heraldic perfection—it was as perfect, poised against the sky, as the mosquito had seemed, poised on his arm. It trapped him with fascination.

Sending out a final sonar note to pinpoint the mosquito, the bat struck its head forward—

But Hector was diving now, under it, swirling in the air, letting himself fall for a ways just to get the most distance.

He glimpsed the hangarlike opening of a window and flew for it. He sensed a body inside and newly flowing female blood. An even bigger woman.

He had to rest first. He found a spot on a wall near the ceiling. Sometime later there was the sound of a radio alarm coming on to wake the sleeper below him, the radio in mid monologue...

And this is the KRED crack-of-dawn-news, all the news that's fit to transmit. Look out for your hamburgers, folks, that's the story that comes to KRED radio from Lubbock where a woman was shot by a burger. It seems that some twisted soul has been putting .22 calibre bullets into ground meat sold at Lubbock supermarkets. The bullet exploded while the burger was cooking last night and the woman suffered a minor facial wound from a bullet fragment...Chrysler has announced two new plant closures and plans to lay off some 35,000 people...Give us about, oh, an hour and we'll give you the first KRED morning traffic report...

When Lulu woke, she had cramps. But it was the aftertaste of the dream that bothered her. There was a taintedness lingering in her skin, as if the nightmare of the giant mosquito had left a sort of mephitic insect pheromone on her. She took two showers, and ate her breakfast, and listened to the radio, and, by comforting degrees, forgot about the dream. When she went downstairs the building manager was letting the ambulance attendants in. They were in no hurry. It was the guy upstairs, the manager said. He was dead.

No one was surprised. He was a junkie. Everybody knew that.

Next day Lulu was scratching the skeeter bites, whenever she thought no one was looking.

Ferret 1993

RECURRENT DREAMS OF NUCLEAR WAR LEAD B.T. QUIZENBAUM INTO MORAL DISSOLUTION

Some boom would wake him, as if the outside world conspired with his dreams.

Just before he woke: the cloud, angry red at its column, would grow to dominate the horizon like a great luminous cerebrum and spinal stalk. And then the white flash and *then* the boom.

BOOM. He'd sit up in bed, blinking through sweat, and the room would be filled with whiteness. He'd wait for the Big Burn. The pain. Death.

Slowly his eyes would adjust and his heart would slow and the sweat would grow cold on his taut face. He'd hear the boom again and realize it was only a semi-truck banging as it hit a pot hole. Or another of the city's congestion coughings.

The flash was only the light of the morning sun, seeming sudden when he opened his eyes (unthinking and yet deliberate, he'd leave his drapes open before going to bed). His bedroom windows faced East Manhattan...But before his eyes adjusted, just as he came awake, half in dream delirium, the light seemed the flash of a hydrogen bomb achieving fruition. It shared some quality with the light at the heart of a naked 200-watt bulb; the cancelled place where, when he stared into the bulb, his eye refused to assimilate color: a heart of whiteness. A throb of almost ostentatious blankness.

It was August. As if August were a kind of Season for them, the sky seemed filled with planes, jets issuing ominous roars; each jet, in Quizenbaum's mind, potentially the bomb-bearer. Every aerial tumble would send him breathing hard to the window.

He wouldn't go to a therapist. The dreams frightened him, but they were fevered, salty melodramas. He didn't want them explained.

"Oh," the therapist would probably say, "possibly the recurrent nightmares of World War Three represent the expression of your sublimated hostility against the world. You're destroying the whole damn world in your dreams, Quizenbaum, because you wanted to be a set designer for the theatre and instead you're an usher. You blame the world itself, the fundamental source of all injustice. You are forty and you know it's too late. You're unmarried and lonely. Understandably, these things anger you." And no doubt another would say "You're a Jew without a heritage, a foster child. Your mother converted to Christianity and then became a drunk when you were five. A year later you were taken to live with Gentiles; and you've always been afraid to go to Temple, afraid of refection. You are a Jew without Judaism, and you resent the Jews because of this. The bomb is your way to destroy the city that seethes with Jews—after all, Quizenbaum, your dreams always take place in New York City. The mushroom shape represents the dome of the synagogue, and the sublimation of your fear of women, which..." And other drivel. Quizenbaum could anticipate them. He had toyed with analysts before and they had left his world more opaque than ever.

The dreams were not identical. Some nights the nightmare included Tricia. Tricia was a girlish woman in her twenties who'd once worked at the theatre, taking tickets. They'd dated a few times, then she'd announced she was going to marry someone named Barry Malstein, because he was a corporation lawyer and because he was Jewish. "I mean," she said, in an apologetic aside to Quizenbaum, "he's *really* Jewish. But, really, you're a much better conversationalist. But, really, I feel that my therapist is right, he says my life is too...um..."

Still, Quizenbaum remembered Tricia fondly. He had not dreamt of nuclear explosions on the single night he'd spent with her.

In the dreams featuring Tricia, they would be sitting together on the veranda, arguing quietly about something. He was never sure what the argument was about. She would stand, as if to leave—and then the sky would darken with the mushroom cloud behind her, like a sort of cobra's hood over her head, and the world would start to come apart around them. Stock footage of natural disasters, buildings swept away by flood, cities buckled by earthquakes. He would sweep her into his arms and, carrying her as if she were made of paper, plunge into the house, the terror fueling him, driving him with a surge of excitement he never experienced when he was awake. The house would become gelatin around them, the walls transparent, the white light suffusing everything. The BOOM would arrive, bringing with it the shockwave. Tricia screaming, the scream lost in the roar. He would turn to look directly into the white light.

That's when he'd wake. When he looked the explosion in its cyclopean eye.

In other dreams, he'd be walking along in a crowd, perhaps leaving a football game (he never went to football games) or a rock concert (he disliked loud music); or he might be one card in the great shuffle of Times Square (he never went there, awake). The cloud would come, the glow. Every head in the crowd, whatever crowd it was, would turn to squint under overshadowing hands at the explosion unfolding. There was a split second, before the blinding light and the shockwave hit them, when they were fused exquisitely in their sense of mutual destiny. Now we're all of us ashes in the same urn, Quizenbaum would think. The glow would increase, the fireball would sunder the horizon, death coming hard at them like a steel mallet descending. He would look the glow in the eye and—

He'd wake up.

But sometimes the waking was incomplete. He would seem to see the crowd in his bedroom with him, thousands of them in a room hardly big enough for four, everyone looking at the window, anticipating the blast. They were insubstantial; people of glycerin. He'd shudder, and the room would invisibly tumesce with air pressure, till the walls were about to burst. Instead, a quiet, sickening *pop* happened in the bones about his ears. Another quiver would go through him and he'd be alone, the hot morning sun making his eyes swim with islands of blur. Once, only once, just after the *pop,* he found the sheet between his legs wet with fresh urine. This discovery brought a kind of euphoria.

✣

In considering the implications of his recurrent dreams, Brent Taylor Quizenbaum had come to certain conclusions. He tried to explain his conclusions to a woman who introduced herself as "Maria—you know, like in *West Side Story?*" in the Nightbirds Bar & Grill. They stood at the crowded bar together; there were no stools. He was pleased to find he could put his foot on a brass rail near the floor. He'd never done that before.

Maria was taller than he was, and darker, and her acne scars glowed in the underworld glamor of the black-light. Half-hidden in tinfoil, the black light was screwed to the ceiling above the topless dancer teetering on a platform behind the bar; she was not quite in command of her clear plastic high-heels. Now and then Quizenbaum's round-eyed gaze would stray to the dancer who, in pasties and g-string, her skin leaden under the black light, was making vertical wriggling movements as if she were trying to squeeze into a dress that was too small for her.

Quizenbaum returned his attention to Maria, gaunt blackhaired Maria and said, "So you see, these dreams, along with certain international indications, have brought me to the conclusion that our world is indeed coming to an end. Civilizations have their life and death cycles. Ours is too absurd to be allowed to go any further. Nuclear holocaust in my lifetime." He paused dramatically. "And in yours, Maria."

"Yeah!" she said nodding, sipping her screwdriver.

How deep her understanding! "So you see," he went on earnestly, "it all links up with the fascination people have for disaster movies and horror movies, and all the desperate, jaded attempts at new thrills—like free-basing and "swing" clubs. These things tell me that, deep down inside, everyone knows that The End is coming." He took a large pull on his own screwdriver; he could hardly taste the Tropicana orange juice for the vodka. A terrible, magnificent lucidity took hold of him. He had never before had so much to drink.

"We all *feel* it coming..." he gestured eloquently, trying to invoke the word. "We feel it coming...*intuitively*. Right?" He turned his magnificent lucidity against her, looking her in the eye.

"Right!" she said, unblinking, signaling the bartender for two more drinks. Quizenbaum paid for the drinks—he'd paid for the previous three rounds.

How *sensitive* she was! Quizenbaum thought. He really liked her. "So, Maria," he went on, settling into the groove of his rhetoric, "if we agree that nuclear holocaust will soon kill us all, how do we cope? How? We've got to live for the moment, till the white light and the Big Burn come. And if it feels right, we've got to live hard and fast and loose...All were expressions Quizenbaum had laughed at till now; he felt as he supposed the dancer above the bar felt, that he was wriggling into something ill-fitting. But when he said, "We've got to let ourselves go and *feel*," he smiled, becoming more comfortable with the clichés. "And then, Maria..." He looked deep into her red-rimmed brown eyes, "we've got to greet the actual moment of nuclear death with...with dignity and...and, uh...*you* know...with euphoria. The sort of euphoria that comes with giving up, joyously. Release at last!"

"Right on," she said, though the noise level in the crowded bar probably made it impossible for her to make out most of what he was saying.

"And there's something more...I know it's all a bit reminiscent of *Doctor Strangelove,* but...when that bomb hits, we'll all die *together*. For once, everyone in New York City will really be *together*. It'll be almost like being in love!" He leaned close to her to hear her reaction.

"Sure as *shit!*" she burst out.

Somewhat deflated by this malaprop phrase, he drank off the remainder of his screwdriver. His head spun, and a wave of disorientation overtook him. A flash of light at the door—it was only a cop directing a flashlight at a dark corner of the bar. But Quizenbaum staggered, for a moment thinking the white light had come.

It wasn't the first time that day; he'd started at sirens (is that an air raid siren?), jets breaking the sound barrier (is that the final BOOM?), mothers screaming at their children (are they screaming "Run for the fallout shelter!"?) Sometimes a silence would startle him—was it the silence prefacing explosion?

He shook himself and returned stalwartly to the bar. "Hey, baby," Maria said, tussling his hair and tilting her head inquisitively. "Wassuh matter?"

He smiled warmly at her. She wasn't sophisticated, but by God, she was *real*. "In the light of our dish—uh, discussion," he said, "don't you think we ought to explore one another while we still can?"

As she took him by the arm and led him out the door, he heard someone at the bar say, "Maria always gettsuh—" And he couldn't hear the rest. She gets the *what?* he wondered.

"She knows what she's doing," someone else replied.

Misinterpreting, he nodded to himself. "Yeah, she can pick 'em," he murmured proudly, the world reeling around him.

He didn't put another interpretation on the remarks he'd overheard till he woke the next morning—fully dressed, on the rug beside his unmussed bed—and found

A) Maria gone.

B) A pool of vomit, likely his own, in the doorway of the bedroom.

C) His wallet gone. It had contained ninety dollars and one credit card.

D) His clock-radio and blender gone.

He made a sound that was something like a bark of laughter. Then he winced. He took three codeine, remaining from an old dental prescription, and went to bed.

The cloud advanced into the sky, and retreated, and came back again. It came and went in pulses. It would advance a ways, its fireball unfolding like a paper bouquet from the wrist of a magician. And then the bouquet would return to its sleeve, the fireball devolving as if on a film run backwards, and people would look away from the horizon, forgetting what had been there, just as if nothing had happened.

The fireball would unfurl again—and it would reverse, the world restored in seconds. "Indecisive jack-in-the-box," said Quizenbaum, who was floating bodiless over the city. Then he was down in the square, somehow apart from the thousands flowing in currents around him, feeling inert and anonymous.

The mingled fear and elation began teasingly when the horizon lit up, the cloud emerging. The crowd would turn and look and, in the terror that united them like hot plastic flowing over everyone, Quizenbaum was no longer inert, no longer anonymous. It didn't last; it didn't quite consummate. He was left with frustration. The film would run backwards, the cloud withering, folding in on itself. The crowd forgot all that had happened. He was again alone.

Quizenbaum awoke in darkness. He had slept the day through. That was the last time he had the dream, in any form. A week later he placed an ad in the Personals section of *The Village Voice.*

The ad was incomprehensible to everyone who read it. But Quizenbaum sat for hours, watching the black telephone.

The ad read:

> BURN TWO AND THEY BECOME ONE. I PROVIDE MATCHES IF YOU HAVE GASOLINE. MORE THAN SUICIDE. CALL ME AT...

One day the phone rang.

Ferret © 1993

JUST LIKE SUZIE

Perrick is in his underwear, standing in the middle of the room, trying silently to talk himself out of slamming crank. He's a paunchy guy, early forties who looks ten years older than he has to, and knows it. He's in a weekly rates hotel room in San Francisco. It's not boosh-wah but it's not a piss-in-the-sink room, as it has a small bathroom. Perrick lives here, for the moment. He's used to these rooms, because he's lived half of his double life in them, but he's not used to *sleeping* in them; not used to the shouts in the hall at night, the heavy tread of cops, the shrieking fights of the two junkie gays downstairs. But this Bedlam is genteel, one of his neighbors assures him, compared to other weeklies on the street.

The room contains, besides Perrick, a double bed, a dresser on which is lined up aftershave, cologne, a box of tissues, a man's comb, a cheap chrome-faced radio. There's a lamp table by the bed, with a squat lamp on it, a wastepaper basket below it. A window onto the street. A raincoat hanging on a hook.

Perrick is alternately pacing and going over to a table on which is a syringe, already filled and capped up, and a spoon. He nervously pokes at the syringe, holds it up to the light, puts it down, whines a little to himself. Of two minds about using it. He picks it up again, puts it down and goes to the bathroom door. He calls through the door, "Suzie! Damn, come on, girl!"

Suzie's hoarse voice from the bathroom: "Just take a fuckin' chill-pill, man, you gotta get your stuff in you so you be a little fuckin' understandin' about me gettin mine!"

"Heroin," Perrick mutters to himself. "Sick bitch. She's gonna give me AIDS or something." He yells at the door again. "Come on baby let's *do* it!

Suzie emerges from the bathroom—she's skinny, with bad skin, thin bleached blond hair, a white girl who's affected a lot of the local homegirl mannerisms, mixes them all up with her white Valleytrash SouthernCal roots. "Your princess is here, dude!" She walks a little unsteadily on her heels, and she's nodding a touch. "You got my money? I paid you when you came in!"

"That was like a down payment thing." She sinks onto the edge of the bed and fumbles a cigarette out from her purse, which is still on her shoulder strap...Her movements become slow and deliberate as she lights it.

Perrick yells, "The fuck it was! I can't believe you pullin this shit after rippin me off last time—my fuckin credit cards—I can't believe I'd go for you again but..."

"OK fuck this, I'm goin', I don't need no accusations, you totally illin, you dissin' me, *fuck* you." She starts to get up, sways, falls into sitting back on the bed. "Shit."

"OK OK fuck it. Here." He slaps more money down beside her, it's gone almost before it hits the mattress, into her purse...then she droops a little, nodding...comes out of it, shaking herself.

"Wow. Shit's good. Let's do the Thing. Before I nod out or

something. You want it like before?"

Perrick nods, unzips his pants, then hesitates, takes his wallet out of his back pocket and puts it where he can keep an eye on it, in the middle of the dresser. Then goes to the raincoat, puts it on over his underwear. Buttons it up. He goes to her, taking up the syringe. Perrick makes as if he doesn't notice her. He's looking at the ceiling and humming absently but breathing rather rapidly.

Suzie, in a practiced little girl's voice: "Oh! I wonder what would happen if I looked inside this big grown-up man's coat when he's not watching me! My *goodness!* I wonder what's in here!"

She unbuttons the bottom button of his coat and puts her head under it. Feels around. "Oh what's this nummy yummy! Mmmmm! I wonder what the big man will do...!"

Perrick gasps as she begins giving him head, her own head bobbing. Perrick snatches up the syringe, drags back his coat sleeve and fixes, registers immediately. His back arches and his jaw quivers as he rushes. Never as good as the first rush he had the first time he did it and every time he does it he feels a little more strain on his heart and he half hopes that this time the ticker goes blooey but still he's riding what rush there is, enough to make him go: "Oh Jeezus oh yes little girl you bad dirty little girl oh yes take it take it oh yes you ripped me off you dirty little girl my credit cards but I forgive you because you are the little girl who loves me loves to oh yes—" Faster and faster as the drug takes hold. "Good crystal good meth little girl you ripped me off and my wife found out and had to tell her the whole story and she kicked me out and here I am can't believe I'm back with you, you caused it, you got me kicked out bad little girl bad little girl..."

His movements are convulsive as he grabs the back of her

head...his repressed anger emerging in the violence of his hip thrusts and hands taloned on the back of her neck. Faster and meaner. She's gagging. Choking. He's oblivious. He's gasping, "...Shouldn't do it shouldn't do it but you made me bad little girl you made me buy the stuff made me buy you made me I didn't want to I don't know what to do how'd I get into it I don't know Andrea left me...your fault your—" He punctuates the words now with vicious thrusts into her. "—*fault!* Your *fault!* Your *fault!*"

She's still gagging, choking, but now only resisting feebly. The heroin was the synthetic stuff, hard to gauge its strength, more than she bargained for.

Perrick's singing idiotically: "Heroin and speed, you and me, heroin and speed, you and me, you down and me up, never quite enough, heroin and speed make her bleed make her sorry she stole from me—"

She's choking more and more. He holds himself deep in her, forcing a sustained deep throat...her struggles are now like mock motions of a sleeper acting out a dream.

Perrick's babbling, "Bad girl little ripoff artist broke my heart take my dick, show you're sorry...SHIIIIIT!" As he orgasms and she...stops moving. He slumps over her. Hugs her to his groin. "Fuck. I'm sorry I got too..." He straightens up, panting. "Hope I didn't hurt you..."

He tries to pull away from her. Frowns. Sees he's stuck or she's not letting go. She's otherwise totally limp.

Perrick muttering: "Said I was sorry. Come on. Let go. You're hurting me. Shit you got my nuts in your mouth too...how'd that—?" Yelling now: "Hey! Suzie? You're hurting me, seriously! What is this, I'm supposed to give you more money or—" He stops, grimacing with clamping pain at his groin. Bending to look under the coat. She's beyond unconscious. He can see the profound emptiness of her. A slackness beyond slack. Already tinged blue. And at the corners of her jaws the muscles are bunched with a signature of finality. She's clamped onto his dick and his balls, both in her mouth, her teeth clamped like a sadist's cock-ring over the root of his maleness. "Jesus fucking Christ! Suzie! Don't be dead, come on, that's a fuckin bitchy thing to do to me! Don't be—" He checks her pulse at her throat. "I don't fucking...She is. She's dead. Shit shit *shit!*"

He tries to ease her off...when that doesn't work, makes an effort, tells himself Stay Calm, as he attempts to yank free. "Awwwwwwwwwhhhhh shiiiiiit! Fuuuuuuck!"

It hurts.

He takes a deep breath. Forces a measure of relaxation into his limbs. Then tries again to wrench her loose.

Searing pain.

He yowls. Then he stands there, panting, feeling the weight of her hanging from his genitals. He's holding her up *by* his genitals. He moves to try to get her head more in the light, then attempts to work his thumbs between her teeth, try to pry her off. Pushes—

Crunching pain. Some sorta death-reflex. She's crunching down harder on him every time he tries to pry her loose. Like punishment for the attempt...

"Owww fuck goddamnit!"

A banging at the door.

He recognized Buck's geeky voice coming from outside the hotel door: "Yo! You got Suzie in there! Say hey you got my lady in there, dudeski?!"

Perrick mutters breathlessly to himself, "Oh shit it's her fuckin' pimp!" Then yelling at Buck, "No, no man she—she split!"

"Hey bullshit! Come on, man! Get over here, open this door!"

Whining, Perrick grabs the corpse under the armpits and drags it along with an awkwardness that seems a weirdly apt choreographic parody of his path through life. When he gets to the vicinity of the door he's got her turned the wrong way, she'd be visible if he opened the door, and there's not enough room for a "U-turn" so he has to bend over—grimacing horribly—and grab her skirt and sort of lift her at the hips, so her back is humped, and he does a little capering hump-swivel-hump-swivel hump-swivel move, till he gets her turned round. He whines some more as Buck pounds the door. Now Perrick's standing sideways with respect to the door, the body behind it. He adjusts the raincoat. Unlocks the door and opens it some—trying his best for fake composure—and opens the door only enough so that he's peering around the side of it.

There's Buck. He's emaciated, his blond hair in a white boy's approximation of dreadlocks. Under his arm's an expensive skateboard with a lot of cartoony stickers on it; he's wearing Levi jacket sans sleeves, stupid looking surfer shorts, tattoos.

Perrick attempts: "Hey. Buck. I paid her, man. She's out hittin the pipe an' hittin the needle, slammin your money."

"Heeeeey Dudeski the bitch does that again she's gonna be a bad memory an' she knows that. And I hope she hears me." He shouts past Perrick: "You hear me, bitch?!"

Perrick is holding her up with one hand to take the weight off his dick and the strain is hacking away at his veneer. Can't take much more.

Was she going to bite through? She can't—she's dead. Right? Right?

Buck's saying, "I bet she's in the bathroom doin up some shit and laughin. I always know when she's laughin' at me no matter where she is. I can feel it. Right now. I'm like, psychic. Her mouth's open and she's laughing right now—

Perrick ventures, "I don't think so." He's walking a line, between whimpering and hysterical laughter. He feels like he has the weight of the planet hanging from his dick. The pregnant mass of the fucking bitch Mother Earth.

Buck ignores him, he's shouting, "—And I'm gonna KICK HER ASS FOR IT!" And he kicks the door, smashing it into the corpse and Perrick so that the pain dances through Perrick and expresses itself with a long ululating howl and he tries to edge aside but the door is kicked again and *wham,* bangs into the corpse again and Perrick howls again, tries desperately to get out of the way until at last Buck pushes in and past him, turns and sees the body with its head under his coat.

"Oh this is cute, right when I'm talkin to you she's givin you head, dude!" He starts yanking at the body to get her out where he can slap her around. "Tryin'-a pretend you're not here, I bitch-slap you, let go of that shit and get your ass over here!"

Perrick is making a hot-coals kind of dance, his face a rictus of pain, trying to prevent his dick from being pulled off—starts following Buck's pull around the room in a Chinese parade dragon effect with the body, making funny little marching shuffles with his feet like a kid playing choo-choo.

Perrick yelling, "No no don't you don't—no wait!"

Suddenly Buck stops and stares. Looks at the body. Lets it fall limp. Steps over to the panting Perrick and peeks into the coat. Takes a startled step back.

"Jeezus! You fuckin murdered my old lady with that puny

little dick of yours!"

Perrick's sobbing, "I didn't mean it, Buck she just—she was all nodded out and I guess I got carried away on some crystal and I guess I was kinda mad at her anyway so I was kinda chokin her and I didn't see what was happenin and—she just croaked, man! And she clamped down on there some kinda deathgrip reflex thing and I'm fuckin *stuck*, man!"

"The balls too?"

"Yeah yeah yeah. Yeah. I really got carried away, you know?"

"This..." Buck shakes his head as if in high moral judgement. "This...this is gonna cost you extra."

Perrick suddenly feels a cold melty feeling at his dick. He thinks, at first, she's bitten right through. But then he checks it out. He sees..."Oh shit. Oh no. I'm losin feelin in it. It's *not hurting.*"

"Well you oughta be glad, dudeski!"

"You don't fucking understand! If I can't feel it—that *means it's dying! MY DICK'S DYING!!*"

Buck crosses his arms, considers the strange union of the corpse and the dick with a philosopher's judiciousness. "Yo, calm down, there's a way...we make a deal, we get you out...This is *so* totally gnarly."

Buck starts moving around, looking at the thing from different angles, sniggering behind his hand.

Perrick yells, "It ain't fuckin' funny, Buck!"

"Sure it is. You know what else? This is just like Suzie. It really is. And you know what *else?* It was in all the signs today, man." He takes out a glass crack pipe, blackened with use, thumbs in a rock and fires it up, poofs in a thoughtful way. Buck's head seems to expand slightly like a toy balloon. He exhales and chatters, "Astrology, it was her planets, man, they're all fucked up with her lunar signs. And it was in the smog colors. You ever read smog colors. Like tea leaves? And the way people was walkin in the Mix, I always know, I'm kinda psychic like that, I see the patterns in the Mix, you know? Somedays there's wack shit in the air that just gets a life of its own."

Perrick's on the gelatinous rim of the Grand Abyss called Hysteria. "Stop hittin on that fuckin pipe and get her the fuck *off me!!*"

Buck blows white smoke and says, "Hey don't be comin at me like that, dudeski, 's bullshit."

"I got a few thousand dollars in the bank, I can get you two hundred fifty bucks right away, get you two thousand tomorrow, you get her off me. It's all I could get out of the joint account I had with my wife when I left her but you can have it all man. Just...Just...shit..."

Buck's interested now. "Two grand?" He looks speculatively again at the corpse: "Maybe I get a screwdriver and pry her jaws or something?"

"No no you do stuff like that she clamps down harder. Some kinda reflex thing or something. And I don't want anybody to get crazy with a knife because *my fucking DICK is in there, you know what I'm saying?* It's still all swollen up, I don't want just anybody cutting around in there—I got to have a surgeon."

"But you go to the emergency room, the cops will come around. I tell you what. I know a doctor. He does bullet work and shit. He'll do it and he won't roll over on you. He's good. But we can't get you to him with that thing hangin' down there and he don't make housecalls no matter what—he don't never go out. He's a speedfreak worsen you. Totally tweakin. But he cuts good. He smells bad but he cuts good..."

"So...what are you saying?"

"Gotta cut off her head."

Perrick stares at him. "What?"

"I'm waiting for another idea, dudeski. Cut off her head first—or, anyway, cut off her body I guess—do it quick, we can get you out of here with it..." He takes a big buckknife from his pocket and opens it, flourishes it...

Perrick hesitates. Hands jittering as he pokes at the head, trying to see how his genitals are doing. "I don't know...It's all purple. Oh God. I...I'm gonna get gangrene. And I gotta piss. I can't..."

Buck suggests, perfectly seriously: "Heeeeey, wait'll we get the head separated from the shoulders, you can piss out her neck." He hits the pipe again.

Perrick retches, at this, a retching from deep inside him...he screws his eyes shut...then he takes a deep breath and manages: "Just...Just do it, just do it. Cut off her...her body. Her head. You know."

Buck laughs, "Me?! No way, Jose! Fuckin *A* no-way!" He folds up the knife and drops it in Perrick's coat pocket. "That's your jobby, kimosabe! I just paid eight bucks for a good organic vegetarian lunch and I ain't gonna lose it!"

Perrick protests, "Hey look, seriously, I can't—"

"You wanna lose your dick? You did her man, it's your fuckin responsibility. I come back later. Oh first—" He takes her ankles. As if to a chauffeur: "To the bathroom, James."

Clumsily, each step risking Perrick's ability to reproduce, they carry her between them to the bathroom. Buck chuckles. "I swear to God this is just like her...I was gonna kill her myself tell you the truth but I'd never do it that way, wouldn't trust the bitch..."

✣

In the bathroom Perrick is standing in the tub. Takes out the knife, then removes his coat and tosses it on the floor next to Buck. Trying not to think about it, he opens the knife and begins to saw at her neck.

"Yo yo yo yo whoooooa!" Buck blurts. "Wait a mother-fuckin minute I wanta get outta here before you..." He backs out of the bathroom, grimacing, heads for the hall door, pauses to take a hit from his pipe, goes out the door stage whispering just loud enough for Perrick to hear in the bathroom, "I'll be back, man, I got to cop some rock but I'll be back, take you to that doctor, a thousand bucks and that's between you, me and the rollers if you don't come through..."

Perrick still sawing. Sawing and sobbing. He expects her to react by biting down harder but—though blood spurts and then levels off, simply wells out of her, she doesn't react and that's horrible. How can morticians do it? Just...sawing at someone. They should scream or something, dead or not. Maybe she *was* clamping harder? There was no feeling down there now. How could he tell? "Oh God oh no. I'm gonna throw up on her. This is...I can't feel a thing now I think I...I think she's biting through Oh God..."

The blood making hollow spatters and dripdrops into the tub. Wet crackly noises as he goes through the spine. Letting his eyes glaze, his hands seem to know the work. CRICK-CRICK-CRACKLE.

SPLURT.

Thump .

The body thumping down onto the tub. He drops the knife onto it. Turns quickly because he can't keep it down anymore: the vomit. Painful vomiting. Then he turns on the shower. Vomit and blood going down the drain.

He steps out, dries himself off—and dries off the head too. It has mostly finished its draining. It's bluish yellow now. The eyes sunken into the head more. Cheeks sunken. His dick, where it shows at the root, above her teeth, is angry red and blue. He wonders if he should wash her hair. Give her a shampoo. What the fuck. Maybe *brush her teeth too* while he's at it.

Crazy thoughts. Control yourself. Walk your ass through it, Perrick.

He steps through the bathroom door with the head dangling from his groin. It bounces ludicrously as he walks. A bloody towel wrapped around the neck stump. The head's eyes are open now and looking up at him. Once more he's wearing the raincoat and underwear. Raincoat isn't bloodsoaked but his stomach is spattered and the underwear is scarlet brown and his legs are streaked. He looks somewhat relieved and yet in shock. Staggers over to his rig, his syringe, draws some crank from the spoon. Looks down at the head. Starts to giggle. Suppresses it.

Says to himself, "Wish I had some horse. Like to take some. Share some with you. Don't worry, I don't have to pee no more, I can't feel nothin down there...Hey...close your eyes, Suzie..." He reaches down and tries to close them...doesn't work...nervous GIGGLE..."OK, I understand, sure: we got to have *some* communication." A peacock's tail of garbage in his head. He thinks: I'm losing it. He looks at the needle. A friend. "Speed ain't right for this. Need champagne for...I don't know if this is a marriage or a divorce..."

He says the Magic Words: "Fuck it." He injects the speed. Rushes. Giggles. Sobs. Giggles. Sobs. Babbles.

"Suzie...Suziebitch talk to me, tell me: is this...this is your way to—"

He's interrupted by a delicate knock on the door.

He hears a fluting female voice, sort of silly flirtatious "Andy! oh Annnn-dyyyy!"

Perrick at first thinks this is Suzie's voice. Stares down at the head. It's pulsing from the drugrush. Emanating.

"Suzie—How'd you say that with your mouth full?" Laughing and crying both as he says it.

The voice again and this time Perrick realizes it's coming from the hall door. "Annn-dyyyyy! The Pakistani lady at the front deh-esk said you were ho-ommme!" A more normal voice: "Come on, open up, hon, let's talk!"

It sinks in who this is. His wife. Andrea. He mutters, "Jesus Fuck. My fucking wife I don't even—but oh yeah sure—sure uh-huh makes sense..."

He starts to giggle and tosses the syringe into a wastebasket, buttons up his coat over the head. Throws a bedspread haphazardly over the small amount of blood on the floor that dripped through the towel. Funny head-hump bobbling under the coat as he goes to the door, opens the door for his fairly straight wife who looks around with distaste. She's Jewish, well dressed.

She says, "This place even *smells* horrible, doll. Listen—" She closes the door and comes toward him. "You look awful. So—you've been using? You ready to come home? I thought about it and thought about it and I don't think you would've gone to that whore if you weren't on the drugs. I mean, you weren't in your right mind, and we're gonna take you to one of those twenty-eight day programs and start over—if you're willing I mean you really have to be willing. And no more women, paid for or otherwise..." She stares at his legs. "Why are you wearing a raincoat and no pants? It's not even raining. You got shorts on under there?"

"No I...Got a head. Ahead of...myself." Trying to keep down the crazy half giggle. "Put on the coat before the pants. Come on, sit down."

Andrea looks around skeptically. "Where? I don't know if I want to sit on any of this...I mean, do you launder any of this bedding?"

"The bed's Ok. Just...*head* over here." Laughter creaking down in his throat as he gestures to the bed. She moves to it and sits gingerly.

"You threw the bedspread on the floor? Very nice."

Perrick giggles moronically. "*Head* to." He walks awkwardly toward her.

"You're walking funny, your shoulders all slumped, you got a back ache?"

Perrick's close to tears now, getting it out spastically. "Got to keep your HEAD down in this world!" Fairly *barking* the word "head." He snorts, "If you don't keep your HEAD down, you've HEAD it, pal!"

She gapes at him. He begins to laugh hysterically. She looks at the lump bobbing under his coat. "Whatever have you got...?"

Perrick is sobbing openly now, breaking down. "*HEAD*N'T THOUGHT ABOUT IT!"

And then the towel dislodges and falls to his feet in a wet bloody lump.

Andrea gives a rabbity little shriek and jumps to her feet. "You've been doing something again. Something..."

Perrick approaches her, feeling madly earnest. Seeing a

crepuscular ray of hope. "Andrea—talk to her. You're a woman. Talk to her for me. Convince her to let go."

It might work. It might.

Andrea just backs away, the bitch, whenever you really need them they pull shit like this...

She squeaks: "What?"

Perrick pleads, "Talk to her! Woman to woman! What do they call it? Yeah: *Tete a tete!* Talk to her—!"

Blood is dripping down his leg...he starts to open his coat...

Andrea bursts out: "You don't have to open that!" She's angling for the door. "You really don't have to. I don't—I mean, everybody should have their personal space, the marriage counselor said that and uh—"

But he opens the coat and flings it off. Andrea's eyes are pingpong balls in her head as she sees Suzie. She takes a long noisy breath that sounds as if she's choking on something...touches her throat with her hand...

Perrick approaches her, weeping, smiling, idiotically appealing: "Talk to her about it, Andrea, just get down there and jaw with her! Woman to woman! If you want to talk to her face to face I could—" He squats and bends over so the head sort of half dangles between his legs...he's quite serious and sincere as he goes on: "—and you could, you know, go around behind me and put your face under me there—if you don't mind, I mean, you always said I had a cute tush—you could just—"

Andrea's backed into the door. She turns and claws at it. Yanks it open with a sound of animal fear and sprints out into the hall. Perrick stares after her, a little disappointed but already forgetting about it. He turns away from the door and begins to caress the head, to move his hips against it, not like fucking but more like...dancing. Then Buck appears at the door, staring down the hall at the retreating Andrea.

"Yo dudeski your old lady's really geeking out behind—"

He breaks off, seeing Perrick dancing. As Perrick dances over to the dresser, turns on the radio. It's playing "CHEEK TO CHEEK." Buck looks ill and disgusted.

Perrick is tenderly dancing with the head, singing along, badly but sincerely. "...when we're out together dancing cheek to cheek!"

Buck murmurs, "Oh wow. Dudeski."

The music swells in Perrick's head. Buck looks at him calculatingly now. Then goes to him, drapes the coat over his shoulders, leads him—still dancing—to the door. "You know what? Your old lady's going to call the cops...let's get out of here...Get to that ATM...I bet that cunt has your bank account frozen but we got another wheeze maybe..."

To Perrick, the part of him that used to plan his life and drive his body about, all this is seen detached, like from behind a trick mirror. He's just watching as he body -dances out the door with Buck. He watches without feeling as it goes along with him down the stairs and down the street.

✣

A vacant lot. A half-dozen neighborhood homies and dudeskis hanging around a lazy blue flame in a rusting oil barrel. One of this group, a black guy calls himself Hotwinner, is arguing with Buck. Saying, "I say it's a load of fuckin bullshit."

Buck shrugs. "Put your money down and check it out. I'm lying, I pay off three to one."

Hotwinner says, "I get to look *close.*"

Buck nods. "Rockin'."

"You got it. Just don't pull any gafflin bullshit—" And he forks over five bucks.

Buck says, "Anybody else?"

Two others pony up. "Yeah here, it's a waste of good wine money but fuck it—you goin' to pay off or we keep you ass fo' my dog to have his dinner—"

Buck yells at the rickety van parked at the curb. "Hey yo, Perrick! Let's do it!"

No response. Buck makes a sound of irritation, hustles to the back of the van, drags Perrick out. Perrick's wearing his long coat over the bulge. Perrick is giggling. Mumbling to himself: "...telling me all the secrets so hard to understand what she's saying sometimes but she knows it all knows it all...she's a Head of her time hee hee..."

Buck brings him to the firelight, pulls back Perrick's coat, exposing Suzie's purulent head still clamped on his dick and balls, one eye hanging down from the skull, dangling next to his testicles, jigsaws of the scalp rotted off, pig bristles of hair remaining, maggots dripping now and then, squirming...halfway to a skull...

"That's a pig head or somethin, that ain't no bitch!" a dudeski protests, but Buck draws him closer, makes him bend and really look. He backs away making phlegmy sounds in his throat as Buck says to the others, "OK, dudeskis, take a good look, you paid for it." A few other people drift over to check it out. Buck covers the head. "Anybody else want a look? Five bucks!"

Buck taking more money, murmuring to vacant eyed Perrick, "This is way cool, the bitch still workin' for me, tha's, like, loyalty to the max, you knooooo? I mean, it's just like Suzie to hang in there, dude...Lemme count the money dude..."

THE MOTHERFUCKIN END

INTRODUCING THE BLACK ICE BOOKS SERIES:

The Black Ice Books Series will introduce readers to the new generation of dissident writers in revolt. Breaking out of the age-old traditions of mainstream literature, the voices published here are at once ribald, caustic, controversial, and inspirational. These books signal a reflowering of the art underground. They explore iconoclastic styles that celebrate life vis-à-vis the spirit of their unrelenting energy and anger. Similar to the recent explosion in the alternative music scene, these books point toward a new counterculture rage that's just now finding its way into the mainstream discourse. The Black Ice Books Series brings to readers the most radical fiction being written in America today.

The Kafka Chronicles
A novel by Mark Amerika
The Kafka Chronicles investigates the world of passionate sexual experience while simultaneously ridiculing everything that is false and primitive in our contemporary political discourse. Mark Amerika's first novel ignites hyper-language that explores the relationship between style and substance, self and sexuality, and identity and difference. His energetic prose uses all available tracks, mixes vocabularies, and samples genres. Taking its cue from the recent explosion of angst-driven rage found in the alternative rock music scene, this book reveals the unsettled voice of America's next generation.

Mark Amerika has lived in Florida, New York, California, and different parts of Europe, and has worked as a free-lance bicycle courier, lifeguard, video cameraman, and greyhound racing official. Amerika's fiction has appeared in many magazines, including *Fiction International*, *Witness*, the German publication *Lettre International*, and *Black Ice*, of which he is editor. He is presently writing a "violent concerto for deconstructive guitar" in Boulder, Colorado.

"Mark Amerika not only plays music—the rhythm, the sound of his words and sentences—he plays verbal meanings as if they're music. I'm not just talking about music. Amerika is showing us that William Burroughs came out of jazz knowledge and that now everything's political—and everything's coming out through the lens of sexuality..."

—*Kathy Acker*

Paper, ISBN: 0-932511-54-6, $7.00

Revelation Countdown
Short Fiction by Cris Mazza

While in many ways reaffirming the mythic dimension of being on the road already romaticized in American pop and folk culture, *Revelation Countdown* also subtly undermines that view. These stories project onto the open road not the nirvana of personal freedom but rather a type of freedom more closely resembling loss of control. Being in constant motion and passing through new environments destabilizes life, casts it out of phase, heightens perception, skews reactions. Every little problem is magnified to overwhelming dimensions; events segue from slow motion to fast forward; background noises intrude, causing perpetual wee-hour insomnia. In such an atmosphere, the title *Revelation Countdown*, borrowed from a roadside sign in Tennessee, proves prophetic: It may not arrive at 7:30, but revelation will inevitably find the traveler.

Cris Mazza is the author of two previous collections of short fiction, *Animal Acts* and *Is It Sexual Harassment Yet?* and a novel, *How to Leave a Country*. She has resided in Brooklyn, New York; Clarksville, Tennessee; and Meadville, Pennsylvania; but she has always lived in San Diego, California.

"...fictions that are remarkable for the force and freedom of their imaginative style."

—***New York Times Book Review***

Paper, ISBN: 0-932511-73-2, $7.00

Avant-Pop: Fiction for a Daydream Nation

Edited by Larry McCaffery

In *Avant-Pop*, Larry McCaffery has assembled a collection of innovative fiction, comic book art, illustrations, and other unclassifiable texts written by the most radical, subversive, literary talents of the postmodern new wave. The authors included here vary in background, from those with well-established reputations as cult figures in the pop underground (Samuel R. Delany, Kathy Acker, Ferret, Derek Pell, Harold Jaffe), and important new figures who have gained prominence since the late eighties (Mark Leyner, Eurudice, William T. Vollmann), to, finally, the most promising new kids on the block.

Avant-Pop is meant to send a collective wake-up call to all those readers who spent the last decade nodding off, along with the rest of America's daydream nation. To those readers and critics who have decried the absence of genuinely radicalized art capable of liberating people from the bland roles and assumptions they've accepted in our B-movie society of the spectacle, *Avant-Pop* announces that reports about the death of a literary avant-garde have been greatly exaggerated.

Larry McCaffery's most recent books include *Storming the Reality Studio: A Casebook of Cyberpunk and Postmodern SF* and *Across the Wounded Galaxies: Interviews with Contemporary American SF Writers.*

Paper, ISBN: 0-932511-72-4, $7.00

New Noir

Stories by John Shirley

In *New Noir*, John Shirley, like a postmodern Edgar Allen Poe, depicts minds deformed into fantastic configurations by the pressure, the very weight, of an entire society bearing down on them.

"Jody and Annie on TV," selected by the editor of *Mystery Scene* as "perhaps the most important story...in years in the crime fiction genre," reflects the fact that whole segments of zeitgeist and personal psychology have been supplanted by the mass media, that the average kid on the streets in Los Angeles is in a radical crisis of exploded self-image, and that life really is meaningless for millions. The stories here also bring to mind Elmore Leonard and the better crime novelists, but John Shirley—unlike writers who attempt to extrapolate from peripheral observation and research—bases his stories on his personal experience of extreme people and extreme mental states, and his struggle with the seductions of drugs, crime, prostitution, and violence.

John Shirley was born in Houston, Texas in 1953 but spent the majority of his youth in Oregon. He has been a lead singer in a rock band, Obsession, writes lyrics for various bands, including Blue Oyster Cult, and in his spare time records with the Panther Moderns. He is the author of numerous works in a variety of genres; his story collection *Heatseeker* was chosen by the Locus Reader's Poll as one of the best collections of 1989. His latest novel is *Wetbones*.

"John Shirley serves up the bloody heart of a rotting society with the aplomb of an Aztec surgeon on Dexedrine."

—***ALA Booklist***

Paper, ISBN: 0-932511-55-4, $7.00